RAJ TAWNEY

PUBLISHING

This is a work of fiction. Names, characters, places, and incidents either are the product of the author's imagination or are used fictitiously. Any resemblance to actual persons, living or dead, events, or locales is entirely coincidental.

Copyright © 2024 by Raj Tawney
All rights reserved. No part of this book may be reproduced or used in any matter without written permission of the copyright owner except for the use of quotations in a book review.

Cover art by Daniela Alarcon
Book design by Amanda Bartlett and Lau Moraiti
Edited by Bobbie Bensur and Saanya Kanwar

9781223188553 English Hardcover
9781223188560 English eBook

Published by Paw Prints Publishing
PawPrintsPublishing.com
Printed in China

For anyone who's ever felt like an outsider.

And for Michelle.

CHAPTER 1

"Brillo head!" Tyler Roth is screaming and ruffling my hair.

Directly in front of me, his cronies — Kevin Park and Jimmy DeMarco — grab my nipples and squeeze. Hard. They twist their wrists and flutter their lips, old airplane propeller engines igniting. This isn't the first time I've received an "Earhart" from them; it started last year after a class lesson on the history of flight. I'd hoped sixth grade would be different. That they'd be over this joke.

"Having a nice flight, Lindy?" Jimmy asks. I can hardly breathe now, let alone answer him.

"I thought it was a Wright brother?" Kevin chimes in.

"No, no. Lindbergh came after the Wright brothers. Didn't you pay attention?"

"Of course I did, idiot!"

"No, you're the idiot, idiot!"

The co-pilots are shoving each other with their dominant arms now; their other hands still grasp my shirt, tightly. I can't help but stare at the old brick walls behind their heads. They're painted in a thick aqua blue coat that's now peeling after years of neglect. It's probably not a good idea to inhale next to paint chips, probably not a good idea to breathe at all with these two and their smelly armpits facing me from either side. Has nobody told them it's time to start buying deodorant?

"You guys are crashing and burning! Eject! Eject!" I squeal and try to squirm away.

"Watch it," says Tyler, snarling. "Remember Christopher Columbus?"

How could I forget? Way back in third grade, when I first moved here, we learned about Christopher Columbus's voyages. And the bullying first began: my nipples were dubbed the "Niña" and "Pinta." I don't feel like mentioning where the "Santa Maria" is located.

Not even halfway through the first day of middle school and they've already started in with me. Tyler and his dimwits had cornered me under the staircase when the lunch bell rang. They saw me walking out of Miss Schyler's math class and told me that they missed me over the summer break. I'm an easy one to spot since I look almost nothing like everyone else in my school.

Funnily enough, I don't look like anyone in my family either. Not my mom or dad, cousins, aunts, or uncles. I don't look like someone who belongs to a specific culture. My skin isn't white nor is it dark. My eyes aren't round, almond, or hooded. My hair isn't straight or tamed. It's super curly and each strand is facing a different direction. I try to be cool with it. It worked for Albert Einstein, right? Right?! Who in the world hated *that* guy? And he had a fun accent, too — kind of like my dad. . .

I grew up being told that I'm special. Parents love to tell us that. Really, my parents are just from different worlds. My dad is from India; my mom's mom is from Puerto Rico, and my mom's dad came here from Italy. I hear all about it at the various family gatherings and parties I get dragged to. Each group is so different from the other. Different clothes to wear, songs to remember, gods to obey, languages to pretend to know, dances to avoid. And the food. Well, the food is the only great part. I get to taste flavors from all over the globe. Lasagna with the Italians, arroz con pollo with the Puerto Ricans, and palak paneer with the Indians. My tastebuds are never lonely, even though I am most of the time.

Whether I'm at school or with my family, I don't see myself in anyone. Period. I'm an olive-skinned, bushy eyebrowed, broken mop-haired, not-so-skinny boy with a first and last name that nobody can seem to pronounce, let alone figure out where I'm from. Kamal Rao, American citizen. Too "other" for the town. And too American for my brown cousins.

"You're so *unique*, honey," my mom frequently reminds me. She married dad after they met in college. His parents sent him here to America to receive a good education but I don't think they thought he'd *fall in love*. Gross. Isn't that selfish of my parents? What did they think their child would look like? Why don't adults consider these things before they get married and have kids?

New York City might be the melting pot of the world but it's an hour away. The town we live in feels so bland, as if nobody's ancestors tasted their own stew once they got to Ellis Island. I always feel like the odd one out, like a weirdly twisted pretzel in a bag of perfect knots.

My chest has become numb after the pilots' third engine crank, but mostly, I'm getting tired of Tyler pulling on me.

"Cut it out already, will ya?!"

"Good idea!" Tyler says. "Kevin, pass me your scissors."

Speaking out was a bad idea. Kevin reaches into his backpack and pulls out a pair of shiny blades. He passes them to his boss. Tyler begins snipping at my hair, taunting me and I hear metal slicing closer to my ear.

"If I take enough off, the janitor can use them to scrub the toilet," he adds, and his two cronies crack up. They each have one of my arms now, holding me back.

I squirm. I squirm and squirm like I've seen the earthworms do in my backyard, whenever I dig a hole and they are exposed to the light. Their entire bodies shimmy in the sun, especially when I pick one up and let it hang onto my fingers. I'd never hurt them though. I just want them out of the way so I can finish shaping one of my mud pies. Their determination to survive is inspiring. I often wonder if they have feelings. Do some worms pick on others? Are some pinker? Thicker? How can they tell each other apart? Maybe that's what the rings on their bodies are for. Do some worms ever feel awkward as they're squiggling around in the dirt? Like they're too fat to fit through clogs of soil, rocks, and tree roots? The life of a worm can't be easy. I've seen bigger animals eat them, from birds swooping down off tree branches to my neighbor's cat Brewster digging for them in the dirt. I know how it feels to have other, bigger species want to slurp you up like spaghetti.

"Why do you have that funny look on your face?" Tyler breaks me from my wormy trance. I'm still staring at the old brick wall and my body's gone limp.

"I— I— I was just thinking about wo—worms," I say.

"Worms? Are you a freak?" he asks.

But before I can answer, something attacks Kevin and Jimmy, and their pants drop to the floor.

"What the—?!" Kevin gasps, his knees knocking together.

"Ah!" Jimmy shrieks. It's squeaky like a dog's rubber chew toy.

Their hands race to their ankles to save their pants. I wiggle free.

"Hurry up!" A voice calls to me from the doorway. The accent sounds familiar, kind of like my dad's, but if he was a kid. I can only see a shadow from where I stand and I quickly bolt to find it, leaving Kevin and Jimmy on the floor, and Tyler consoling them. Suddenly, my savior and I are two blurs running down the hall. When we cross into the lunchroom, safe amongst almost a hundred other kids, I sputter out a "Thank you," and immediately keel over to catch my breath.

I slowly raise my head. A skinny, dark-brown boy with messy pin-straight black hair is standing in front of me. He's wearing a faded, oversized red T-shirt, baggy blue jeans, and a big, goofy smile.

CHAPTER 2

✝✵★

"Did you see their undies?" he asks in that not so unfamiliar accent (except I've never heard it at school). "Polka dots! Mickey Mouse!" he laughs, holding his stomach. "Some tough guys!"

Something is different about this kid. He doesn't seem worried that Tyler and his crew might come looking for him to give him a de-pantsing. He extends his arm for a formal handshake, like I've seen adults do when they greet each other.

"My name is Jaz. I am new."

"Jaz?" I thought I was hearing it wrong.

"Yes! Like the music but with one 'z.'"

I quickly slap his palm. He stares at his hand for a second, confused.

"Um, cool. I'm Kamal. You know, like a camel."

"Not Kuh-mahl?" he asks.

"Well, yeah. But nobody says it that way. They all call me a camel. . . or humpty."

"Humpty?"

"Yeah, like camel humps."

"Oh!" He doesn't seem too quick on jokes. "Yeah, they sure do! You should have seen the one my father used to milk!"

I stare at him for a few seconds, trying to make sense of what he just said. "Did you say milk?"

"You've never had camel milk? It is delicious!"

"Where did you say you were from?"

"I bet your mama and papa say Kuh-mahl, sweetie baby pie." His fingers pinch the air as if pinching cheeks.

"Well, sort of, but even they've stopped trying to say it that way."

"It is a great name!"

"It. . . it is?" Nobody ever complimented my name before, not even Mom and Dad. "Thanks. I like your name, too," I tell him.

"From now on, I will call you Kuh-mahl, like the way our forefathers intended."

"What forefathers?"

"Of the world! Duh!"

I laugh more now. How could I not? He's like a

stand-up comedian, except he's not being cruel. Not like Tyler, Jimmy, or Kevin when they make jokes, which are hurtful. Jaz doesn't seem like he's trying to be a jerk. He's not trying to be anything.

There aren't many brown kids in my school, just a handful. The brown kids? They are trying to be something. They all dress like little mocha GAP ambassadors, slicking their hair in gel, only associating with kids who do that, too. Jaz, on the other hand, has the makings of an F.O.B., aka "Fresh Off the Boat," an immigrant who very clearly isn't from here.

One time, I tried to sit at lunch with Soren Patel, the "hottie" of the "bruppies," a.k.a. the brown preps. He looked over at me and said, "You don't belong here, Camel. Go find a trough." That really hurt my feelings. When we were younger, he was much nicer to me and I admired him, like a brother. Now, he ignores me when we pass each other in the hallway between classes. I don't exist to him. In the cafeteria, the bruppies sit at a big circular table, left of center to the yuppies (same style except all these kids have white skin) who own the middle table. The yuppies are the nucleus of our ecosystem. Or a black hole, depending on how one sees their presence. The two cliques don't interact for some reason but they could. They're all trying so hard to be cool; they could have their own tween drama show on the

WB Network. The colognes they all started wearing this year smell so strong, they could make you dizzy. I usually sit at one of the long benches near the exit door and keep to myself, trying not to be noticed, not that anyone — especially Soren — would.

"Would you like to eat together?" Jaz holds up a white, plastic supermarket bag with what looks like a can inside, weighing it down.

"Sure," I say.

"Sweet. Lunchroom—march!"

He speedwalks ahead of me as if we're in a race. When we had first pushed open the double doors to the cafeteria, he used both hands, wild with confidence. Facing the crowd, he had placed his hands on his hips while the doors swayed back and forth to a close. Now, he's approaching the rows of lunch tables as if they are soldiers, waiting for his command.

He quickly hunts down an empty spot, further inward from my usual section, and plants himself directly in the center. "Kuh-mahl! Here! I found one!" He announces his discovery loud enough for the entire room to hear, even with the dozens of mini conversations going on all around. I even see Soren turning his head in the distance to see what's going on.

Laughter scatters. My cheeks turn red but I keep my head down and forge on. I take a seat on the bench across from Jaz, empty my lunch bag, and unwrap my sandwich from its tin foil. Mom had sliced leftover meatballs for me and put them between two pieces of bread. Then, she added some hot sauce in the middle, just the way I like it.

Jaz removes a can and a metal spoon from the plastic bag, and places them on the table. Refried beans. He pops the top off using the finger slot, digs the spoon in, and shoves a pile of the brownish bean glop into his mouth.

"Mmmmmm." GGGGGUUUULLLLPPPP. He crams in another scoop. "So, where are you from?" he asks while chewing, his words muffled.

"I'm from here: Long Island."

"Really? Always? Your name does not sound like other American names."

I sigh. "I get that a lot. My dad's from India. Mumbai, to be exact. And my mom is from here, the city. Her mom's family is from Puerto Rico and her dad's is from Italy. They wanted me to remember my heritage. Kamal. My middle name is Anthony. It's all very complicated." I hear myself nervously rambling to get the explanation out. I've become too used to describing myself quickly.

"Whoa, that is cool!" He jumps up, bits of bean sputtering from his mouth. I'm surprised by his response — nobody ever told me it was cool to be mixed.

"It is?"

"I knew there was something special about you!"

I smile and shyly bow my head down to hide the blushing on my cheeks.

"You must have a colorful house. Do all the different parts of your family get along? I imagine so many dance parties."

What a thing to say. I guess the different sides don't really love each other. I had never really thought about it. "It's a normal house, I guess. We're not much of a dancing family." I think of my mom then, cooking and playing Gloria Estefan or The Beatles on our little radio next to the stove. Stirring, swaying from left to right, singing along. My dad in his recliner next door in the living room, the TV blaring. "There is a lot of cool food, though. Do you like spicy stuff?"

"Do I?!" I wish these beans were spicy, even though my butt probably does NOT. The kids sitting near me in seventh period would not be happy." He giggles and shoves another spoonful into his mouth.

"Is that your entire lunch?"

"This? Oh, yeah. . . Um. . . My mom did not have time to make me anything. It is okay."

"Do you want half of my sandwich?"

"Really?" Jaz stares at my meal surrounded by tin foil. He looks like he's about to drool. But then he looks more closely and changes his mind.

"Oh, no. I do not eat meat. Thank you."

"You don't?" I look down at my sandwich, feeling awkward about eating it now.

"Please, eat. It looks tasty."

"Well, okay then." I pick up one half that Mom had cut evenly down the center and take another bite.

"So, where are you from, Jaz?" I ask again.

"I am from Pakistan, India's neighbor! Well, we used to be one nation. But Muslims and Hindus hate each other, and there was a war, and we ended up starting our own country, blah blah blah. I am sure you know all about it."

"'Blah, blah, blah?' Wait, wait, really?" How come I never knew about this? My dad almost never mentions his younger days or India or the history of his people . . . well, half of my people.

"You did not know? Technically, Kamal, we should not be friends. We should be mortal enemies!"

He presses his fingertips together, creating a ball shape, like an evil cartoon nemesis would. Then, boom! His fingertips explode and he flaps back dramatically. I pause, holding my sandwich in my hands. I stop chewing. It's probably not a good idea to say war and enemies at school right now. And pretend-explode. The September 11th attacks were only a year ago; people are still sort of scared of that kind of talk, even if it's a joke. Plus, does he really think we shouldn't be friends?

"Kidding! That was so long ago! Of course we can be friends!"

I feel. . . relief? But then a question: "Why would we be enemies anyway if we used to be one country?"

"My grandpa used to tell me about these wars between Hindu and Muslim people. It was complicated. People were fighting over land and what gods they worshiped. It was bad. My family had to move north when they drew the new lines. Yours must have moved south or just stayed where they were."

"Wow, that does sound complicated. All because they were different from each other?" I feel like I've been thinking a lot about people's differences lately. "Maybe we can change things. . . by becoming friends?"

"That is a great idea! We can show Pakistan and India that friendship rules." We high-five over the table, our palms slapping hard with excitement.

Over the past few years, I've gotten used to feeling like the odd worm out in the mud ditch. I've gotten used to being my own best friend. But still, this conversation with Jaz feels nice: talking to another kid who isn't laughing at me but is trying to make me laugh. I don't care what Jaz looks or dresses like. He doesn't care about *Dawson's Creek* or Abercrombie & Fitch. He is real. And it's enough to make me not care about the fact that, together, we're bound to be bullied even more than if we were apart.

"By the way, Jaz. Where did you learn English? It's really good."

"At school. It is mandatory, like learning arithmetic. Did you know Arab people invented math? Well, Mesopotamians, which are like our ancestors."

"Wait, wait, so your teachers taught you to speak English? That's kind of like when my kindergarten teacher asked me if I spoke English on my first day of school. I'm like, 'Um. . . it's the only language I know!'"

"The principal asked me that question this morning — if I could speak English."

"Principal Snyder? Were you upset?"

"I said, 'Of course, I do!' My dad used to bring home VHS tapes of American movies before I even learned English in school. My first words were 'I'll be back' and 'Yo, Adrian!'"

I chuckle. "So, when did your family arrive in—"

"—Do your nips still hurt?"

"Ummm. . ." I look down toward my chest, then back at Jaz. "A little sore, I guess."

"I remember the first time I got a purple nurple. It was from this kid back in Karachi, where I grew up. I was hanging from the monkey bars when he popped up in front of me and TWISSSSSTTTTTT! I fell to the ground, on the hard gravel rocks, and cut my knee."

"Ouch, that must have hurt. Why'd he sneak up on you like that?"

"Because I said Allah was stupid."

"Why did you say that?"

"Why not?" There's frustration in his voice now. He bows his head down towards the table, staring deeply into the laminate wood grain, as if he's ashamed to beg the question.

"Oh." I don't know what else to say. I'm not too familiar with Islam, other than when I overhear Mom and Dad watching the news.

It's silent for a few moments. "We call them Amelia Earharts," I finally tell him.

"What?"

"Purple nurples," I say. "We call them Amelia Earharts." And then I mime it all for him, what those nimrods did to me. I pinch my fingers and pretend to twist and twist; I flutter my lips.

He laughs. And then: "Hey, want to see some naked ladies?!"

He doesn't give me time to respond and whips out a wrinkly Macy's catalog from his backpack. He scoots near me and whips to the bra section.

"Look! Look! Oh, mama!" He points to the women wearing lingerie. I guess he doesn't own a computer. Then again, mom and dad put parental control settings on our computer's internet browser.

I nervously pan my head around the room to see if anyone is staring at us. Not even a head-turn. We are untouchable.

"How much do you think each one weighs?"

It's the dorkiest thing I've ever heard an eleven-year-old boy say about a woman, but he doesn't seem to care if he sounds ridiculous. I smirk, and together we look on, surveying the women in their underwear, considering his question.

Then, I see Principal Snyder approaching. "Quick, put that away!"

Jaz quickly closes the catalog and stuffs it down his T-shirt. The principal is coming closer and closer to us. She stops in front of our table, using her pointer finger to tip her glasses to the edge of her nose so that her eyeballs can look deep into our souls. She's pretty for an adult but wearing a boxy black suit and old lady perfume that makes my nostrils itchy. My throat lets out a loud gulp. She nods at me, then turns to Jaz.

"Hello, Jaz. I hope you're enjoying your first day." She smirks but it looks sort of phony as if she knows we are up to no good.

"Yes, ma'am. I am having a great first day. And look, I made a new friend already."

He puts his arm around my shoulder. His friend.

"I see. Very good. Well, have a nice lunch, boys.

Jaz, I'll check on you again soon."

We both smile our innocent-boy smiles as she slowly walks away and through the double doors. Then, we both let out the air from our chests.

"Do you think she shops at Macy's?" Jaz asks me with a serious look on his face.

We both burst out laughing at the same time. I haven't felt like this ever.

CHAPTER 3

Only one more class to go before the end of the day: U.S. History. I stand at the open doorway while everyone piles in and peek in before entering. No sight of any bullies in this one. I'm actually excited. I love learning about my country and how all of us (well, except Native Americans) come from somewhere else. I honestly think a lot of people forget that.

Sometimes I wish we could learn by doing. All the places to travel. Sites to see. Food to eat.

Sometimes in class, I daydream.

I'll think about what's for dinner and what assignments Mom might give me at the kitchen counter. She won't let me chop the onions yet but I love peeling garlic cloves. Or I'll try to guess how many hours it would take to swim across the Long Island Sound before reaching Connecticut. On a clear day, I can see New London from Sunken Meadow Beach, so how long could it possibly take? I'll stare around at my classmates and often wonder why it seems like everyone's ancestors are from the European continent. Just Europe. Why do we only really ever learn about Europe? Why do we never talk about places like Puerto Rico or India? Except only when we talk about explorers — like Christopher Columbus — and where they landed or what they discovered. What's so great about them anyway? I guess they were brave. I wonder if they were ever scared, the explorers. All alone out there in a new land, far away from everything they knew.

  I wish I had the guts to bring all this up in class. It'd be interesting to talk about. But last year, when I raised my hand during a lesson on the origin of St. Valentine's Day, Jimmy pinched at my love handles from the seat behind me, shouting, "You've got enough love for everyone!" Loud enough for EVERYONE to hear. The whole class laughed. And I felt like crawling underneath my desk. I don't talk much in class anymore.

  Suddenly, I'm jolted forward by a firm slap on

my shoulder. I leap like a frog and turn around quickly.

"Hey Kam! We are both in this one. Should we go in?" It's Jaz. He's wearing a half-moon smile across his face. The same one I left him with after lunch ended. I'm relieved to see him instead of one of the three goons we escaped from earlier.

"Oh, It's just you," I utter, the trembling fading away. "Ready to learn more about your new home?"

"It is me!" he says. "I know a little. I know about George Washington. And Hilary Clinton. George is on the one-dollar bill. My dad told me he was the first president of the United States. And Hilary was always on the TV when my parents were watching CNN. Mom used to call her 'that poor woman.' She didn't look poor to me."

"She was the First Lady a few years ago."

"Like, ever on Earth?"

"No, not ever. That doesn't make sense."

"Then why was she poor? Wasn't she married to the president?"

"Maybe your mom meant she just felt sorry for her."

"Why would she feel sorry for the First Lady? She was married to the president!"

"Good point. Let's just go sit down." I don't want

to sound stupid. I don't know enough about politicians yet. To me, they're all just a bunch of adults barking like dogs on the TV while my parents argue about who's more annoying.

We walk into the classroom together. Most of the spots are already taken, so I lead us to two open desks in the front — not the best seats in the house because now we're right under the teacher's nose. But we have no choice.

"Okay, class, settle down," says Mr. Wright. I already know his name, not just because I'm holding the class schedule in my hands but because he just finished writing it in big letters on the chalkboard. I wonder if he's related to Orville and Wilbur. "This year, we'll be exploring the history of this great land of ours: the United States. And so, we must go centuries back in time, to the time of our forefathers."

I turn my head to the left, where Jaz is sitting. His face lights up, staring toward the front of the room. Then, his eyes scan the walls on either side of our desks. A map outlining all fifty states. One of North America, from Canada all the way down to Mexico. There are also laminated copies of the Constitution and the Declaration of Independence taped to the bright blue painted brick above the chalkboard. Everything seems so exciting to him.

"Can anyone tell me who our first president

was?" Mr. Wright asks the entire room.

Nobody raises their hand. But I know one person who has the answer.

"Oh! Oh! I know!" says Jaz, sitting straight up in his chair, his arm raised as high as it can go.

"Yes, you." Mr. Wright points right at him, delighting in not having to force an answer out of anyone.

"George Washington." Jaz says proudly. I can feel some of the kids staring at him, annoyed at both his eagerness and his otherness.

"That's correct. Good job, Mr. . . . um . . ."

"Rafiq."

"Mr. Rafiq, thank you." Mr. Wright walks over to his desk to check off Jaz's name on his attendance list. "Now, class, did you know that almost every one of us stems from somewhere else? Even George Washington's family came from England! Our nation was founded by immigrants, and they fought for the right for all people to enter this land in search of freedom."

Jaz's smile remains as if hot-glued to his face.

"How we enter America, however, has changed over the past two centuries. Even the past century. The past fifty years. Heck, even the past few years," Mr. Wright continues. And with each passing sentence, his words become less teachery, less upbeat. He's sounding more. . .what is it? Annoyed? "We all came here for one reason or another, from across the globe, most of the time escaping hard times in other countries."

Jaz nods his head, solemnly.

"More important." And he says this part more to himself, walking back to his desk to grab the full attendance list. "We did it proudly. We didn't sneak in, like some people do now."

Was that directed at us? I'm sure only us two in the front row hear it. Mr. Wright had said it so lowly and so randomly, I hardly believe he did say it. But Jaz's smile and head-nodding suddenly stop cold. He must have heard it, too.

Mr. Wright's voice is back now, louder, more in control again. "Now, class, how about we go around the room and introduce ourselves. One by one, tell me where you come from. I don't mean this town or state. I mean your family. Where did they start out before landing in the good ole' U.S. of A.?"

Jaz remains still, as solid as an action figure.

"How about we start with you, Mr. Rah. . ."

I am frustrated for my new friend. There's no reason our teacher should forget how to say his name already. This guy is supposed to be on our side.

"Mr. Rah. . . Fack," Mr. Wright finishes, still staring at the attendance list. He nods once, feeling good about his attempt, and looks to Jaz expectantly.

"Well," says Jaz. "Well, I am. . . from Pa-Pa-Pakist-an. . ."

I can't figure out why he's acting so spooked. Annoyed, I can understand. But why scared? Only an hour earlier, he had de-pantsed some bullies on my—a stranger's—behalf. He had spilled his whole life story to me at lunch. He was confident. Proud. Was a dumb grown-up really going to get to him?

"Ah, Pakistan. They're going through some difficult times. And when did you and your family arrive?" Mr. Wright asks.

"We've been here for a while. Loads of years," Jaz explains, crumpling his schedule in his hands.

"Very good." Mr. Wright says. His eyes then drift over to me. "And how about you, Mr. . ."

"Rao. Kamal Rao." I respond swiftly.

Mr. Wright checks off my name with his pencil. "Go ahead, Mr. R-ay-ohhhh," holding my last name for a few extra seconds.

"Well, my dad is from India. Bombay — or Mumbai now — to be exact. He came over here decades ago as a student," I explain as quickly as I can.

"And your mother?"

"My mom is from New York City."

"And where is her family from?"

"Um, her mom grew up in Puerto Rico and her

dad is from Italy. . . We're all over the place! Like the United Nations!" I blurt out nervously, shrugging my shoulders. I am half-joking but it's not getting any laughs. Everyone, including Mr. Wright, is close mouthed. Jaz looks like he is holding his breath. For a beat, the only sound I think I hear is air coming from Mr. Wright's nostrils. He is unsure what to say.

"All over the world," I clarify, clearing my throat of nervous phlegm. "And America too, of course." For some reason, I feel like I need to reassure him.

"Mutt!" A voice calls out from the back of the classroom. Anonymous. The rest of my class giggles.

"Woof, woof!" Another kid adds. More laughter. I blush. My heart races.

"Settle down, class. Settle down. That's inappropriate," says Mr. Wright, anxiously. "Let's move on, shall we?"

As each student speaks, it's pretty clear my hypothesis is correct. Their entire family is from Ireland or Scandinavia or Russia or Germany. Or sometimes "I don't know." But I bet I can guess. If you look at a globe, you'd have to spin it all the way around before you'd find all three places my family is from. I feel alone in that thought, even though I'm an American like everyone else. I think about what Mr. Wright said at the beginning of class. Centuries. My family didn't have centuries here.

The bell rings, signaling the end of the day. Thank goodness. All the kids begin to flood into the hallway and through the exit doors. I head for the bus and see Jaz sitting on a bench by himself at the side entrance.

"Hey, Jaz! I didn't even see you leave class." I'm hovering over him now. But his head doesn't lift. I want to tell him I'm sorry. Sorry for suggesting we sit in the front row of U.S. History, just to sit together. Sorry for the way Mr. Wright asked him weird questions in a weird way that obviously made him feel sad and small. I knew the feeling, too. Instead, I just say: "Great first day, huh?"

"It was. . . okay," He replies. He's still looking down.

"Just okay? Come on! You saved me from those jerks! We checked out ladies in bras!"

I see his shoulders ease and I imagine that half-moon smile creep back.

"And guess what? I made a new friend, too."
"You did?"
"Yeah, you!"

There it was. That smile. Taking up his whole face. All teeth. Then, a thought comes to him. He digs into his backpack and takes out the crumpled Macy's catalog, slips it to me from behind his back. "Here," he says. "This is for you. Shhh! Open it on the bus, okay?"

I don't want it. I don't know what I would do if my mom caught me with it. But I feel like I can't say no to him. I swipe it quickly, as if it's stolen merchandise, as if we're doing something illegal, and I quickly push it down into my own backpack under the pile of notebooks, pencils, and my gym socks.

"Thanks," I say. "Are you getting on a bus?"

"That one over there." He points at the other end of the parking lot to the last few buses in line."

We high-five and go our separate ways. I climb up the bus steps and head straight for the very last row. Plop down. I feel exhausted. I look out of the window and watch Jaz walk off into the crowd, getting smaller and smaller. I can't make out which bus he gets onto.

Once my bus rolls off, I reach into my bag and pull out the catalog. I'm not sure why. I guess I can't help myself. I turn to the underwear section, the same page we were gawking at when Principal Snyder spotted us and find that Jaz has drawn all over the models' faces. He's transformed them into cartoon characters with funny eyes, ears, and mustaches, all with the flick of a thick, black Sharpie. On another page, underneath three ladies in lace nightgowns, he's written "TYLER. JIMMY. KEVIN." I belt out loud with laughter. So loud. A couple kids flinch but I don't keep their attention. At the bottom of the last page: "HAVE FUN, KAM! YOUR FRIEND — JAZ."

I laugh and smile to myself and I don't even care how crazy I look laughing and smiling in my empty part of the bus, a bird alone on a branch. I can see a new world from where I sit, and my eyes are wide open. So much to discover and I know it's hard to do that when you're flying solo. Every bird needs a flock. Maybe I'm finding mine or learning how.

I lean my head against the window and stare out to a sea of houses, wondering if Jaz lives in one of them.

CHAPTER 4

✟※☆

It's a few weeks into the school year. Both Jaz and I love Spider-Man comic books and telling stupid jokes, and playing outside in the dirt during lunch hour, and pretending — as we walk the halls between classes — that we're not really kids at all but spies on adventures far, far away from this place. Jaz is the best. He isn't afraid to raise his arm high when he knows an answer in class, and he cracks up over the lamest things that people say sometimes, and he's decorated his locker with dozens of these cool stickers of wolves howling at the moon. And every time he opens it, he howls a little too. He's so weird! But so am I, and it feels great.

What he lacks in street cred, Jaz makes up for in cleverness. Like this morning, during homeroom (turns out we have the same homeroom!), he's building an entire miniature house out of folded notebook paper, unsharpened number two pencils, and a wad of used gum he found under his desk.

We're sitting around waiting for the bell to ring. Everyone else is talking, mostly about boring stuff like shows on the WB or which teacher they think has the biggest butt. A few are sleeping at their desks, snoring. Not us. I'm watching Jaz delicately stack long, hexagonal "logs of wood" to create one wall, then balance more pencils in the other direction, to create a corner. He's sticking pieces of the gum in between connecting ends to hold the walls together. His concentration is intense; he barely breathes. And with only five minutes to go before the bell rings, he's completed an entire square building. Some of the more curious kids begin to crane their necks to look at his handiwork. And then, seeming unimpressed, go back to their talk circles or their naps.

"Where did you learn to do that?" I ask him.

"It passes the time. When the electricity is out."

"Like, in your house?"

"Back in Karachi, we lost power a lot. I got good at making forts, too."

"I do the same thing when our power lines go

down during a storm! Except I make forts in my room using blankets and pillows." An idea pops into my head. "Hey, we could try to build one in my backyard after school today? I play a lot in the woods behind my house. There are a ton of sticks and leaves to make a fort. And I can get sheets from the laundry room. We can sleep out there sometime."

"I love to sleep outdoors!" Jaz says. "Can we make a campfire, too?"

"Maybe. I've never tried to make one before. Don't you need matches? Or a lighter?"

"I can show you. I saw my father make plenty of fires. It is not hard."

It's a general rule in our home that we need to ask permission before having anyone visit (even Grandma Clarita!) but there isn't time to ask. It's Friday, and Mom is bombarded with meetings and my dad is at interviews all day. I can't borrow the front office phone to try and get them. Even if I could, they'd want to know everything, learn all about Jaz first. They always think kids around my age will steal their expensive stuff for some reason, like Mom's jewelry or our DVD player, even though I try to explain to them the kids I know aren't like "city" kids my aunts are always going on about. I don't know how to explain Jaz to them anyway. He's not either, really, a city kid or a suburban kid. Plus, it's been a long, long, long time since I've had a friend over. I've obviously outgrown the neighborhood kids: the wannabe athletes who always leave me in the dust on the school track during gym class, the same ones who can seem to do a thousand pull-ups without ever getting tired when I can barely even do one. I don't want to explain it to them.

I decide I won't have to. My parents won't be home till 6:30, at the earliest. And I'll make sure Jaz is gone by the time they get home.

"We'll meet at my bus," I tell him.

Then, Tyler comes over and, in one swoop, smashes Jaz's house apart with his math book.

"Is that where you live, F.O.B.?"

A half-hour after the school day ends, Jaz and I are already rushing off the bus and toward my house. It's an Indian summer; the sun beats down on us and sweat trickles down our necks and arms, which are covered by fall jackets. Mine, a fleece my grandma got me. His, a black I Heart NY windbreaker.

"Hey Jaz, let's go round back," I tell him.

He raises both thumbs into the air, then sprints across our lawn ahead of me.

I meet him in the backyard where our freshly

mowed, half-acre of grass sits before the untamed woods that stretch for a good while. During the day, the woods are always exciting to enter. I imagine I'm in a jungle and exploring unknown land. But during the night, I get totally freaked out by the pitch blackness. One time during the summer, I had been roaming back there for way too long, and the sun began to set. It got dark while I was still in deep, and I got lost clawing my way out. I ended up tripping over a big, dead tree trunk and fell into a wild thorn bush. By the time I finally found my way to our back door, I was scraped up pretty bad. Mom screamed. She thought I had gotten into a fight with a raccoon and wanted to rush me to the emergency room to check for rabies. I told her what actually happened and she took me into the bathroom to dab me a hundred times with rubbing alcohol. It was my turn to scream then. The rubbing alcohol felt like a thousand bees were stinging my body. That was the first, and last time, mom let me wander in the woods without her knowing. Well, until today.

It was a good lesson for a city kid. My family had only moved from Queens when I was eight; that's where I first learned to explore. Where there's concrete everywhere: buildings, sidewalks, playgrounds. We didn't have much nature in our old neighborhood. Our apartment building was part of a row of buildings that looked just like ours. When I played outside, it was mostly on a hard surface. I tripped and fell plenty on the cracks in the pavement, scraping my knees too. Thorns are painful in a different way. A bigger way even.

Still, I don't miss the city at all. Even though there were more kids with darker skin in my last school, I found it hard to make friends there, too. I learned to have my own fun without friends, camping out in my bedroom under the covers, pretending I was in the middle of a forest. It's almost like my imagination wished for a new home because when dad got a new job, we packed up and moved to the middle of Long Island, into a house at the base of a gigantic forest. Dad tries to tell me it's only some brush that hasn't been built on yet but to me it's another world. A happy world.

When I approach him, Jaz is gazing at it all, amazed. And it makes me smile. "This is all yours?" he asks me.

"Yep," I say proudly. "Wild, isn't it?"

"Yes!"

Jaz and I cross over the lawn and enter the woods. We pick up twigs and sticks of all sizes, feeling each one for their weight and length. After about ten minutes, we run back to the grassy clearing, just outside of the thicket. We dump armfuls of broken branches on the ground in front of us. His pile looks a lot bigger.

"Whoa! That's impressive." I say excitedly.

"Thank you! I helped my father build an entire tent using what we found in the fields outside of the city. Right after we left our home."

"You mean you lived in it, too?"

"After he lost his job, my parents couldn't afford our old home anymore. So, we traveled a lot." He sees I am sad for him, and he waves it away. "It is okay, Kamal. Being hungry sometimes stunk but I got used to the rumble down there."

My dad recently lost his job too but we're still in our house somehow, and our refrigerator remains full of food. I can't help but wonder if we may end up like Jaz and his family, homeless and hungry. I try to put my own fears out of my mind. It's not the right time to tell him about my family's problems. I want him to have a place to unload—his sticks and his feelings.

"What about school?"

"I missed a few months. After that, we ended up here."

"How?"

"On a boat and stuff. . ." He is no longer looking at me. I'm afraid I've upset him. But then, he grabs for a particularly long, gnarly twig. "Hey, look! This stick is also a wand! Ta-da! I'm Harry Potter and you are Ron Weasley!"

Jaz separates his feet into a wide stance, holding out the stick as if he has some incredible power. For a second, I almost believe he is about to perform real magic in front of me, this kid who has known what it's like to wander, to go hungry, to make fire. I'm also impressed that he knows who Harry Potter is. I quickly grab a stick too and mirror his stance. We raise our wands high, and hoot and holler until we collapse to the ground, laughing so hard our stomachs hurt.

We're lying down, gazing at the clouds and trees. Then, we're sitting up, staring into the woods.

"Lions and bears! Oh my!" He's gotten the quote from the *Wizard of Oz* wrong but it's okay. We just laugh and laugh. Lions and bears. Really, our woods are full of squirrels and raccoons that like to pick through our garbage cans for leftovers. Still, I love nature. I keep the TV on Animal Planet when I'm home because I'm just so curious about different creatures. From lions to wolves to elephants, they all seem to do similar things: hunt, play, clean, sleep, and look out for their family. And the ones who eat other animals never kill more than what they need. Humans don't seem to do that. "They all live in harmony," Mom likes to remind me whenever she sees me glued to the screen, watching something about the rainforest or the ocean. "They're all mixed up," I agree.

Two hours later and the sun is starting to go down. We finish constructing the two walls that will help assemble our makeshift tee-pee-fort-tent-house-thingy. Jaz shows me how to weave the branches together like a basket. We each hold a wall that extends beyond our wingspan and lean them against each other to make a near-perfect triangular shelter. Then, we toss an old sheet that I had found in our pantry earlier over the top to fill in the holes. It's amazing seeing our campsite come together.

"We did it!" I cheer.

"It was not that hard!"

Then, I hear Mom's car pull into the driveway. I know it is hers by the loud noise her old engine makes. Dad is always trying to fix it himself but it never takes too long for the engine to act up again. A pit forms in my stomach.

"Wait here," I tell Jaz.

I rush inside through the screened back door and greet her as she comes through the front foyer.

"Hi, Mom. How was your day? Why are you home early?" I know I sound nervous. I feel guilty.

"Honey, you're all dirty again. Go clean up. Dad will be home soon. We'll do leftovers tonight."

"Can my friend come for dinner?" I abruptly ask.

"What friend?" She's partly annoyed by the

last-minute ask. Partly curious and happy about the 'friend' bit.

"His name's Jaz. He's. . .out in the back. We've been building this fort out of branches from the woods."

"Why didn't you tell me?" She replies sternly, her attention now on the back door in the kitchen. "You know you're not supposed to have anyone over without my permission. Or go in the woods without me knowing!"

"I know, I know; it was a last-minute thing. I am sorry."

"You never mentioned him before."

"He's new. His family just moved here from Pakistan."

Mom looks confused, her head tilting to the side, rubbing her eyes as if to get a better look at me. But she also looks tired. Always tired. I can tell she doesn't want to say anything dumb out loud but all that rubbing is starting to turn the skin around her eyeballs red.

"Okay," she says with a deep breath. "He can stay for dinner but make sure he calls his parents to let them know."

I run back outside to ask Jaz if he wants to eat with us. He's inspecting our tent, searching for any loose ends.

"Hey! You hungry? My mom says you can stay for dinner if you want."

"Really? Yes. I would like that."

We play a little while longer, till it's newly dark, then Mom calls from the kitchen window: "Dinner! Come wash up."

We pass through the kitchen where she's spooning leftovers from plastic containers.

"Mom, this is Jaz. Jaz, this is my mom."

"Hi, Jaz, I'm Celia. It's so nice to meet you."

Jaz sticks out his hand to shake Mom's. She leans back for a second, then smiles and accepts his hand. It's too bad it's covered in dirt, and by the time she pulls away, so is hers.

"Wash up in the bathroom, boys," she tells us, sighing and wiping her own hands with the kitchen towel.

"Come on, Jaz," I say. "Bathroom is this way, down the hall."

He looks around our kitchen curiously and follows me through our living room. His eyes move all over the place, studying everything, our framed family photos sitting on top of our piano, to the colorful artwork on our walls and the cultural artifacts, from an elephant Lord Ganesha statue to an old Frank Sinatra vinyl album mom has on display in the bookcase.

"Wow, I feel like I'm in a museum," he says. "Your things are so beautiful."

I've never thought much of the old junk in my house. It's mostly family heirlooms given to my parents by their parents, aunts and uncles, and cousins. Mostly ceramics, paintings, glass plates, and wooden figurines—all with stories I've heard repeatedly at family gatherings. Like the porcelain Buddha that my grandpa had in his home back in India—he flew all the way across the globe to bring it to us. Dad loves retelling that story. Its purpose is to bless our home. I think of him every time I pass it. I only met him a couple of times, once when I was a baby, which I can't remember, and the second time when he visited us when I was about three years old. He was a sweet, old man. I wish I had the chance to know him better before he died.

Jaz rubs the Buddha's stomach. It starts to shake back and forth.

"Stop, Jaz! You're going to break it!"

"You rub his belly for good luck. Come on, try it."

He takes my hand and places it over the statue which is still unstable. I pull away and try to stop it from falling to the floor.

When it stops moving, I let out a sigh of relief

then turn to Jaz. "If this thing breaks, you'll never be allowed back here again."

"Now you have good luck."

"How do you know about Buddha anyway?"

"They are found in Pakistan. It is not just Muslim people there."

"But I thought India is all Hindus and Pakistan is all Muslims?"

"Why would you think that? Both countries have Hindus and Muslim people. You see that Ganesha statue next to the Buddha? I've seen one back in Karachi, too."

"Really?" I'm surprised. The little bit I know about India and Pakistan is that they don't like each other's religions. I've overheard adults at parties talking about how they don't like Pakistanis but they never explain why.

"There is a story behind everything, Kamal."

Jaz is right. There is more to things than just what we see. Maybe we do that to people, too. I know I've felt that way.

We wash up and head back to the kitchen where Dad is now sitting at the table, halfway through his first can of beer for the night. I give him a hug and a kiss on the cheek.

"Nice work out back, boys."

"Thanks, Dad. The credit goes to Jaz."

"Hello, sir." Jaz bows, then offers another formal handshake.

Dad softly chuckles to himself. "Pleasure to meet you, Jaz. I'm Rishi."

"Your home is beautiful, sir."

"Thank you. The credit goes to her! I just live in it." Dad lifts his chin in Mom's direction. It sounds like a compliment but really I know he's saying it a little meanly. Mom rolls her eyes. It goes over Jaz's head.

Mom is finishing up heating the last of the leftovers as we take our seats. She sticks serving spoons inside each bowl. Jaz examines the various dishes, looking slightly confused. Mom helps make sense of the spread, pointing to each one.

"These are from a few dinners we had this week, Jaz. This one is chicken and potato curry. Here you have rice mixed with pigeon peas. Spaghetti and meatballs in that one. Kidney beans doused with Sazón seasoning over there. Also, the naan bread is a little cold, so let me know if you need it reheated. Please, help yourself."

Jaz's eyes open wide. Fear or excitement? I'm not sure which.

"Jaz doesn't eat meat," I explain to Mom.

"That is okay, Kamal. I can just eat the other stuff."

He grabs a serving spoon and digs in, adding a little bit of everything to his plate. Rather than one small bite at a time, he mushes all the foods and flavors together, then throws big spoonfuls into his mouth.

"This is delicious! I have never tasted anything like this in my life!" He cleans his plate, then he serves himself seconds. My parents look both pleased and horrified as they watch Jaz. Somehow, his hands and shirt are covered in food, and he makes a lot of noise while he chews. Leftovers have always been my favorite idea of a meal, too. Just like mud pies, I love mushing things together. Except I realize, a little guiltily, that I actually *get* to eat leftovers. Jaz is the first kid who doesn't make me feel awkward about enjoying food. He's just as passionate as I am. I feel proud to have my friend sitting at our table and enjoying my family's cooking.

"Jaz, did you remember to call your parents?"

His cheeks are full, making it difficult to hear his response but he nods his head, even though I know he hadn't called home. I don't want to call him out for lying in front of my parents. They've just met him. I don't want them to find a reason not to have him back over.

"Jaz, you're from Pakistan?" Dad says as he cracks open another beer.

In between large swallows, Jaz finds time to speak more clearly. "Yes, sir. A city called Karachi."

"I've heard great things about Karachi. Our family is originally from that side of the subcontinent but we were forced to leave after the war. Moved to a different part of India."

We did? We were? Dad never mentioned this to me before.

"That is a shame, sir."

"It certainly is," says Dad. "We come from a beautiful part of the world. We shouldn't treat each other as enemies."

"Yes."

"So, when did you arrive in the states, Jaz?"

"A long time ago." Jaz has his head down, clinking his spoon on his plate.

"When?" Mom chimes in.

"A long time ago," he says again. "I have been in New York for only a little."

That's odd. Why doesn't he tell them he came here for a better life? Just like my dad.

"So, what brought you to New York?" asks Dad.

"My father got a new job."

"Oh! Where does he work?" Mom asks.

"Funny" Dad interrupts. "That's how we ended up in this house. I was transferred from the city out to Long Island. And now I have no job. But I do have a mortgage to pay!"

The beer is starting to kick in. After two cans, Dad starts to get mopey and say strange things.

"We're staying afloat, Rishi." says Mom, annoyed now.

Dad looks down at the can in his hand. "Yeah, afloat. The American dream."

"Afloat like a boat." I add. My joke does nothing. The room is silent.

"Where do you and your family live?" Mom asks, breaking up the awkwardness.

"Uh, we live near the King Kullen supermarket. Next door."

"You mean the Mayfair apartments?"

"Yes."

"I thought they closed them up." says Dad.

"No. Lots of people live there."

"And how are you liking your new school?" Mom continues.

"I was not sure I was going to like it there, but Kamal made me feel welcome."

Mom and Dad both smile.

"That's sweet, Jaz."

Ugh. I can't believe she's saying that, like I'm a sad charity case. I feel my cheeks getting warm.

"Kamal is the coolest kid I have met in this whole country. Maybe even in the world!"

I turn to Jaz. "I am?"

"You love playing outdoors, you have all of these cool cultures, and you are super nice."

My cheeks keep heating up but I'm also half-grinning now. "You're really cool too, Jaz." I say, staring at my plate.

"What time are your parents picking you up, Jaz?" asks Mom.

Jaz begins eating again, shoveling it all in, not leaving enough space in his mouth to speak. He's making grunting noises as if he's trying to say real words.

"I'm sorry. Come again, honey?"

Sweat starts to pool at his hairline. He wipes his face with his shirt sleeve then pushes his chair in.

"I really must get home now. Thank you so much for dinner. It was delicious."

"Wait, how are you getting home?" Mom looks

worried.

"I will walk."

"I'll drive you," Dad says, starting to rise from his chair.

"You can't drive," Mom interrupts.

"Of course I can."

"You've been drinking. You can't get behind a wheel."

"I've only had two!"

"Two is enough."

Before they finish bickering, Jaz takes off. My eyes are on my parents but I hear the door squeak open in the living room. I run to the front door to catch him but he's not there, and I can't see anything beyond the streetlamp two houses down. It's too dark.

CHAPTER 5
*༒ ✹ ★ ✶

I wake up in a daze, wondering if last night had really happened. Questions about my new friend roll around in my head. Did he get home okay? Why was he so nervous? Was he keeping something from me?

I wander downstairs to the kitchen where the overwhelming smells of fried eggs and black pepper enrich the air. Almost every Saturday morning, Mom prepares my favorite breakfast: two sunny-side up eggs with hand-rolled lolis, Indian flatbread made of stretched, spiced dough that's dropped into an oily pan to fry. Plus, a tall glass of pulpy orange juice. I look forward to this special time of the week, just

Mom and me.

Dad is already out for the day, playing cricket in the park with his Indian pals. They'll chug beers in between points. It's a weekend ritual for him, something he says he needs now more than ever, with all the stress of a job search. Non-Indians enjoy stopping to watch them play the game because they haven't seen it before. Dad likes to remind me that cricket is as popular as baseball in other parts of the world, and they use a bat to swing at a ball, too, except their bat is flat instead of a cylindrical and their ball is made of something super, super heavy and covered in a glossy leather shell. He's been playing since he was around my age, back in Mumbai, and has taken me to the park before to watch him play with his friends. The game is a little slow and boring but when Dad pitches, he's like Pedro Martinez out there. It's amazing to watch. Sometimes I wish I was athletic like he is but I have a hard time concentrating during sports. I also get out of breath very easily. I wonder if Jaz knows cricket. Do they play it in Pakistan? Maybe I should bring him with me next time I go to watch Dad play.

I sit at the table and watch Mom roll the atta (dough) with her hands, chop onions and radishes, add them into the mound, then flatten it all till it's paper thin. A heated pan on the stovetop is waiting for her. When she lays the dough inside, it SSSSSSIIIIIZZZZZ-

ZLLLLLEEEES and oil splashes a bit. Sometimes, she lets me help her. It's so much fun, like working with Play-Doh. But you can cook it, and then eat it.

She isn't her usual Saturday self. Usually, weekend Mom has gotten some sleep. She'll hum a song while she cooks but today she's strangely quiet. I plop down in my chair at the table, the one closest to her, and she doesn't even turn around to greet me.

"Good morning," I say.

"Did your new friend get home okay last night? Did you call him like I asked you to?"

"Yes." I can't believe I'm lying to her again. I hadn't. I don't know his phone number. Sometimes I think she worries too much. But I must admit, I am worried about Jaz, too.

"Good. He's a nice boy but a little odd. I can't help but wonder how he and his family arrived here."

"He already told you. His dad got a new job."

"Yes but that's not what I mean. I am talking about immigrants, Kamal."

"Weren't we all immigrants at one point?"

"Yes," she says, her voice leaning in the air. Her back is still facing me. She puts the spatula down on the counter and hunches her shoulders. The pan is still sizzling. Outside, the sky is blue and shining.

"Never mind, Kam. Let's not talk about it. I am glad he got home okay."

"Jaz is great, Mom. He gets me. He is a good friend. So what if he's a little different? Aren't you always saying that's good?"

"I'm sorry, Kam. Let's drop it. You hungry?" She picks up the spatula and turns back toward the stove.

I'm feeling irritated. What's the big deal about immigrants anyway? Ever since the 9/11 attacks, I keep hearing the word more frequently, at school and on TV. It's like everyone's become afraid of newcomers, especially if their skin is darker or their name sounds funny. Everyone is afraid of brown people. Adults always sound nervous when they talk about them, like they're comic book villains.

Mom puts a plate in front of me and tells me to eat up. That she doesn't want to hit traffic. Some Saturday mornings, after cleaning up the floury mess from breakfast together, Mom and I jump into her rusty, old Buick Regal and journey over the Whitestone Bridge so I can visit with Grandma Clarita for the weekend. She lives in the Bronx, which might as well be another continent, far away from our small suburb. I treasure these trips.

Once aboard the S.S. Regal, Mom is the captain, navigating over paved frontiers as we embark from our home on Long Island through the Cross Island and Cross Bronx expressways. Before entering the Bronx, we cruise over the enormous bridge, which seems to float on its own, high above the Long Island Sound. I always feel scared as we get closer, ducking under the back seat each time we drive over the Whitestone. My mom gives me a head's up, like a pilot preps passengers for liftoff: "Okay, Kammy, here we go," she says as we enter the on-ramp. I worry that the car will drive right off the edge and into the dark blue Atlantic. Somehow, we always reach Grandma's apartment safely and without seaweed sticking out of the windows.

Grandma lives on the bottom floor of a tiny, old house; her landlord lives upstairs. He is a quiet, old Italian man who likes his privacy. She's been on her own ever since my grandpa died when I was a baby. I never got to know him but Mom loves telling me stories about her dad.

Grandma was the first of eight siblings. They arrived here from Puerto Rico when she was only a toddler. She helped raise her brothers and sisters in a little apartment, with aunts, uncles and cousins all living within a few blocks of each other. And they were always around. I guess that's why she likes living alone now. I have cousins on my Puerto Rican side, but I don't really fit in with them — especially now that I've moved away. Plus, they speak Spanish, and I can't. They can speak English but they prefer speaking in Spanish. My Indian cousins do the same thing with Hindi.

At least once a year, Mom asks Grandma Clarita to come live with us but Grandma always refuses. It stinks not seeing her often. Sometimes I think she's the only one who gets me. Well, before Jaz arrived anyway. She's the sweetest person and I love spending time with her, whether we're watching an old black-and-white movie or I'm helping her cook in her tiny kitchen (but only if she asks me for help). She doesn't fuss over me like Mom and Dad. She just lets me be me and I really do look forward to these weekend visits.

When we parallel park in front of her building, she is already standing on the curb, waiting to squeeze me like a stuffed animal. She's not a tall woman, about the same height as me. She's round and squishy, and her light brown hair is super curly and wavy. The curlers that stick to her scalp each night might have something to do with her hair's texture. Sometimes I lay my face in her fluffy hairdo when we hug — it's a comfortable place to rest. Everything about my grandma is soft and comforting.

Mom doesn't stay too long. She brings me in, takes a spoonful of Grandma's lunch, black beans still simmering on the stovetop, and raves like it's the first time she's ever tasted it, helps to change a lightbulb, and then goes to retrieve her sneakers by the front door. "Have fun, you guys. Don't get into too much trouble." Mom gives me a peck on the cheek. "I'll be back tomorrow afternoon to pick you up, Kam."

There's no time to be lazy and sit in front of her old, wooden TV set that looks like it was built for the Mayflower. It's not even noon yet and Grandma's already preparing an early dinner. Italians always eat dinner around three on weekends, she tells me. Grandma isn't Italian, of course, but she married an Italian man and pretty much considers herself one. She once said, "My skin is fair enough to pass for one, too." For some reason Grandma rarely mentions her heritage; she never speaks Spanish around me or mentions her homeland. Her rice and beans with pork, a recipe she had learned from her mother, is delicious. But she cooks it only sometimes. A lot of the amazing dishes I eat in her home are full of pasta and tomato sauce.

"Kam, baby, are you going to be my helper today?" she asks.

"Sure!" I'm always honored when Grandma asks me, which is only on occasion, and I never turn her down. "What are we cooking?"

"Spaghetti and meatballs."

Inside her small, cramped kitchen, Grandma knows exactly what she is doing at every moment. She is a maestro, moving effortlessly from drizzling oil into the heated pan to sprinkling a pinch of salt into the pot of boiling water sitting on the stove. There are no measuring spoons or cookbooks. "It's all about the feel," she tells me each time I cook with her.

As we work side by side, rolling raw meat into balls, she shares stories from when she was young, but only scenes set in New York. She chops the onions and tells me about the first time she ever saw color television. I peel the garlic cloves and try to picture Lucille Ball's bright red hair appearing before Grandma's eyes for the first time. I could listen to her speak for hours and never get bored. Then, she tells me a story she's told me before. How her parents didn't want her to marry my grandpa, and how his family felt the same, but how they ran off to City Hall and did it anyway. Their families didn't speak to them for years. Not until one Christmas, when she begged them to come over for dinner, so she could announce that she was having a child — my mom.

"I was so anxious," she explains. "When I finally told them, one of your grandpa's aunts said: 'I hope they don't turn out dark.' I was nearly in tears but I tried not to let it show that it bothered me."

I stop rolling the meatball. I stop breathing. I hadn't heard this part before. Why would someone, especially a family member, say that about a child? Plus, what's wrong with being "dark" anyway? Dad has dark brown skin. My cousins on both sides do, too. How could that possibly matter?

"But you know what won them over? These meatballs," she says pointing down to the bowl, raw meat covering her knuckles. "They all shut up and stopped any nastiness once the food was served. From that point on, all they could talk about was how tasty my meatballs were. That's when I knew how to enter their hearts." She says the last part so firmly, thumbing her chest with force.

I look down at the rows of thick, meaty balls that we've placed onto the baking rack. She adds cheese to the top of each one. Suddenly, I imagine each one having a voice, each one a family member saying nasty things to my Grandma when she was just trying to share something wonderful. I'm not sure this is a happy story, even though they loved her food.

"So, they just started liking you and being okay with everything because of your meatballs?"

"You don't bite the hands that feed you." She holds up her two meaty palms in front of me and smirks. They kind of look like mine when I'm playing in the dirt. I smile. I don't fully understand what she means but somehow, I think I can start to see it.

"And now," she adds, "both sides of the family get along just fine. We all still get together. Even with your grandpa gone. Sometimes, it doesn't take much to appreciate people. You just need to open your mind. And stomach." She points at her round belly and we both laugh.

※ ※ ※

On Sundays, waking up in my grandma's apartment is like what I imagine rising out of a cozy cocoon feels like. Even if I'm just on her living room fold-out couch bed, even with its metal springs poking into my back the whole night. When I wake up in her living room, the sun slants through the windows and makes most of the greenish brown furniture and matching carpet appear orange and bright. And I can see particles swirling in the air. And everything is at once strange and familiar, not sleeping in my own bed and yet I feel at home. I lay and stretch out on the couch and think of Jaz, wondering if he and I will ever get to camp out in our newly built tent-fort-thingy. At school tomorrow, what will I even say to him? I still have no idea why he lied and then ran off.

I sit up as the smell of coffee wafts across my nostrils. I can now see Grandma sitting in her recliner, dressed in her purple floral nightgown, trying to quietly crunch down on a burnt piece of toast. The TV is on mute.

I stretch my arms to the ceiling, let out a big YYYYAAAAWWWWNNNN, and rub my eyes. Grandma giggles and whispers, "I didn't want to wake you," before lifting her cup to take a slurp of the steaming hot coffee. I slink out of bed and crawl quietly along the carpet over to her chair and sit by her knee. She strokes the top of my head, and we are both quiet for a few moments.

"Would you like some mango juice?" She knows how much I love mango juice and that Mom can't ever find it at our local supermarket. There's always a bottle waiting for me in the fridge.

I tell her yes and she creaks out of the chair to fetch me some. Once she hands me the glass, she tells me we better get the day of fun started. "But first, we should head to Pammy's." She sounds cranky about it, a chore.

My aunt Pamela, or Titi Pammy, as we sometimes call her, is my grandma's youngest sister. Nearly twenty years younger, she is closer to my mom's age than my grandma's. She lives in the South Bronx with her husband Héctor who probably drinks ten times more alcohol than my dad. He's always asleep in the bedroom when we stop by their apartment. They don't have a lot of money and never seem to leave their block. I admit that for me too, stopping by their place feels like something we *have* to do once in a while. Most times, I'm not even allowed inside. I just sit in the car with the doors locked until Grandma returns minutes later. But they usually send back a plate of tostones for me to take home.

After eating, we get into Grandma's car, an old station wagon with wood paneling on the sides, and we head towards the South Bronx. When we hit a red light, she tells me, "I don't like coming back here." It's something she tells me every time we drop by Titi Pammy's on Sundays. Red lights. Hands gripping the steering wheel tightly. She sighs. "We grew up down the street from where they live now. Ten people in a single room. I practically raised Pammy. Thank goodness your grandpa came along, and I got out before having your momma."

As we drive down Pelham Parkway, crossing over the railroad tracks, the buildings start to look dirtier and some are empty, the windows boarded up. And as we ride down the streets, the colors of the people turn from overwhelmingly white to a mix, white, brown, and black. The stores have bars on their windows; police cars are parked every few blocks; groups of men hang out in the street, rolling dice with one hand and holding dollar bills in the other.

When we pull up in front of Titi Pammy's apartment building, there is a group of men standing outside near the entranceway. Grandma squeezes the steering wheel tightly one more time, with both hands.

"I'll be two minutes."

She reaches into her purse, pulls out a blank envelope, and slips it into her coat pocket.

"Here, take my bag and put it under your seat."

She opens her door and steps out. I hit the lock button and pull the recline lever. Then, slowly, I crane my neck to peer through the window. I watch Grandma walk quickly to the entrance, push the buzzer with her fist, and wait till it buzzes back to let her in. Meanwhile, the men standing around the doorway stare at her. Once she steps inside, they go back to doing, well, nothing, I guess. I keep glancing at them as they drink from bottles stuffed inside brown-paper bags, blasting music from a boombox, yelling and laughing loudly.

One guy, wearing a black hoodie, sees me looking and starts to walk over. My heart paces and I recline back again, listening for his feet.

"Hey, you!" He knocks on the glass. All shadows.

Knocking and breathing. Looking up, I can see the silhouette of that brown-bagged bottle.

I'm freaking out.

"Hey! Hey!" His voice gets louder. Fists pound. His breath forms a residue on the window.

It feels like this goes on forever. And then, I hear a voice: "Stop that, will ya? You'll scare him."

A new shadow. Grandma. And she's. . . hugging the attacker? They step away from the window to allow for some light. When the man takes down his hood, I can see it's just Tío Héctor. I had thought it was a much younger guy. It's hard to tell with the hoodie. Grandma taps on the window and gestures for me to unlock the doors.

Tío Héctor waves at me and grins. "Hola, Kamal. ¿Cómo estás?"

"Good!" I tell him through the glass, waving back. I let out a big sigh of relief as Grandma gets back behind the wheel and we begin to drive away.

"I haven't seen him in a couple years," I say to Grandma. "He looks. . . tired."

"Age will do that," she says.

"What was the envelope for?" I ask her.

"A little money to help them pay their rent."

"Doesn't Tío Héctor work?"

"No, he doesn't, baby."

"Why not?"

"Because, well. . ."

I can tell she doesn't really want to answer the question but I ask again.

"Because, you know, he's out of work. He can't work."

"Why can't he work?"

Grandma looks all around her, as if she wants to make sure the coast is clear. Then, she leans in and speaks softly. "He's not a legal citizen, Kammy."

"He's not?" I whisper.

"He can't work. Not steadily, anyway. It's getting more dangerous out there to do under-the-table work for too long. Cops are cracking down."

"Why doesn't he become a citizen then?"

"It's not so easy."

"Can't someone help them?"

She puts her head in one hand, her fingers massaging the wrinkles on her forehead.

"Sometimes, I wish they'd all just go back to where they came from. All of them."

I can't believe my ears. My warm, loving grandma is speaking down to other people —her own people. I've never heard her say anything like this before.

"But immigrants aren't all bad, right?" Mom's

words from yesterday morning are echoing in my head.

"No, of course not. But some, like our Héctor, came here illegally. And trust me, they're not helping matters. It's hard enough for people like us to make our way in this world here."

"What about Dad? And your parents? And you? Aren't you all immigrants?"

"Yes, Kam, but Héctor broke the law by coming here illegally and then making a family with your Titi Pammy. They're making the rest of us look bad."

"To whom?"

"The people who didn't want us here to begin with, baby."

All this talk about who deserves to live in our country and who doesn't. People are so scared and don't trust others. Why are we all living this way? I thought we were all supposed to be free?

"What happens if Héctor is caught? What will they do to him?" I ask.

"They'll probably deport him back."

"To Puerto Rico?"

"No, Héctor is Cuban." She puts the car in park at a stop sign and takes a deep breath as she stares ahead into the distance. "Listen, Kam. Forget we came here, huh? Forget what I said. I'm tired. Didn't sleep well. I shouldn't have brought you anyway. Your mom hates it when I do. I just really needed to give Titi that money. Their landlord said they couldn't be late again."

She carries on. She doesn't mean what she said. She's stressed. So much news. All bad.

We drive and drive and she carries on. Tries to take it back. But my head is swirling.

Illegal.

Puerto Ricans. Cubans.

Muslims.

CHAPTER 6

✝※★

Monday morning, just before homeroom. I see Jaz and am unsure of how to approach him. He looks busy, shuffling things around in his backpack, bent down beneath his locker. He pulls out a rolled-up cloth and sticks it on the bottom shelf. It almost looks like the carpet underneath our coffee table in the living room but this one is much smaller. Odd. I don't care. I am just relieved to see my friend. But I am anxious to talk to him.

"Hey!" I croak from down the hall. When he sees me, he frowns and looks from side to side.

"Oh, hey. . . Kamal." He's feeling awkward. I can tell.

"Um... what's that for?" I say and point to the cloth, trying to both diffuse the tension and satisfy my curiosity.

"Oh, this? A prayer rug."

"A prayer rug? Like, a rug for praying with?"

"Not with. On. You lay this out on the floor and do your prayers. It is a Muslim thing. We are supposed to do it five times a day but it is hard to find a place to pray during school. I usually find a spot on the floor in the janitor's closet or the boy's bathroom. If nobody is around."

"Why do you have to pray so many times?"

"To keep us close to God, so he looks over us and stuff."

"Does it work?"

"Hard to tell. Sometimes... I guess." He pauses and I see that same hurt in his face that I noticed in the cafeteria that first day we met. "Sometimes" swirls in the air like a bug until, once again, Jaz makes light of it all. "Sometimes... I sit Indian-style and hover above ground, like Aladdin."

"Wha?" I say gullibly. "Um, I don't think you should say 'Indian-style'."

"No, of course I cannot do that. I thought I was the newbie?" Jaz laughs.

I turn red, my cheeks burning.

"How about 'legs crossed?'" he adds.

We both shrug.

"But that's how they do it in the movies, yes?" he asks. "The other day, Kevin Park saw me with this under my arm and asked if I just came from a 'magic carpet ride.' I told him if he gave me five dollars, I would let him take it for a test drive. So, he shoved me into the wall and said, 'No thanks, freak.'"

"I guess he didn't give you any money."

"I tried! I learned that from my dad. He is a great salesman. He can talk strangers into buying anything. A cow, gold necklaces, two-in-one VCR-DVD players."

"I thought he built things?"

"Well, yes. He has had a lot of jobs. Anything for a profit! Even the prophet!"

"Huh?" I'm totally lost now.

"Just a little Islam joke! Come on."

"Wait. Having your prayer rug in school doesn't make you feel. . . I don't know. . . Like, you really don't care if kids make fun of you? Like what Kevin did?"

"Why should I? I am used to being made fun of. Even back in Karachi."

"Kids were jerks there, too?"

"Of course. Why let them bother you?"

Jaz was far wiser than me, I was realizing. I mean, he had to be. He's been farther than I ever have. I wish I was less fragile, like him.

"Wait. Before we go into class, Jaz. About Fri—"

DDDDDIIINNNNNGGGGG

Jaz grabs my hand and pulls me into homeroom. I don't get any other questions in. No probing to learn what makes him so strong, so fearless. No questions about Friday night. It'll all have to wait.

※ ※ ※

By the end of the day, my head is so crowded with lessons and noise and bells ringing and kids cackling that I don't have it in me to make a big deal out of Friday evening. Whatever his reasons, Jaz had to leave. And he is safe. He is okay. So, what if he fibs every now and then? Why do I care? I try to push it out of my mind. Instead, I keep replaying our conversation from the morning. The ease in which Jaz had said "Why let them bother you?" The half-crescent moon smile spreads across his face. And I think about how much better it is to have him in my corner, how awesome it would be to have a friend like him join me at the next "friends of the family" party Dad drags Mom and me to each month. The next one is this Saturday.

They are always so lame, these parties. Usually at the home of some rich guy Dad went to college with and even newer friends he's met playing cricket.

My life is either spent with the wealthy or the poor, and neither are normal. These guys always have gigantic, white houses in the super fancy parts of Long Island. And their kids aren't usually friendly. A lot of the time, they make fun of my clothes and ask awkward questions like: "So, which one of your parents is brown again?" when they already know the answer. I'm usually left out of playing Sega or Nintendo, or half-court basketball games on their lighted driveways. I'm an unwelcome vegetable forced on their plates. The broccoli of the group. I never have a good time but maybe if Jaz comes with me we'll make our own fun.

As we walk out of class, I put my arm around his shoulder. It's weird, I need to get on my tippy toes to do it. "Hey, buddy. Want to come to this boring party with my family this Saturday night? My parents are making me go. Free food, b-ball court. The people are loaded. Lots of rich people stuff to play with."

"Really? That sounds unreal! Your parents are okay with me going?"

"Of course. Why else would I be asking you?" Great, there's another lie.

"They still like me? Even after how I ran out during dinner?"

At least now I know he feels bad for how he took off that night. "Yeah, yeah. They don't care. My mom said you're a 'nice boy.'" Technically, she did say he was. "But make sure you check with your parents first, okay? We can pick you up from your house. What's your address?"

"I actually don't know the address. It's the apartments next to the King Kullen, remember? Pick me up there?"

"Pick you up at the supermarket?"

"It's easier than trying to memorize an entire address, isn't it?"

"I. . . I guess so?"

* * *

The rest of the week is pretty normal. Saturday evening, my family pulls up in front of the King Kullen entrance, waiting for Jaz to appear. As if it's a perfectly normal thing to do. Mom and Dad are silent. They're mad at me for springing the news on them at the last minute and they are still unsure of how to feel about Jaz. Picking him up at a random grocery store doesn't help. When I told them ten minutes before we left, they couldn't back out. If we didn't show up, he'd be standing there all night, I had said.

But it looks like that might not be a problem.

After about ten long minutes idling in the fire lane by the sliding doors, Jaz is nowhere in sight and my parents are starting to get really upset.

"This is ridiculous," Mom says to Dad. "We really should—."

It's now that Jaz decides to surprise us. Jumping from the shadows and in front of the beams: "Here I am! Ta-da!"

He's wearing an oversized, light-blue, button-down shirt tucked into baggy khaki pants and dirty New Balance sneakers that look too big for his feet. Where did he get his clothes? As he climbs into the back seat next to me, his eyes scan the car like he's never been in one this nice before.

"Whoa, is this a limo?"

Dad laughs. "Yes, at your service, Mr. Jaz."

"Buckle up, boys." Mom says.

Jaz glances at me. He looks confused.

"Seat belt, Jaz. Put it on." I tug mine with both hands.

"Oh, yes!" He fumbles around, searching for the buckle. He's clicking and clacking around to lock it in. "Got it!" he says proudly.

"Thank you for inviting me, Mr. and Mrs. Rao," he says, loudly enough for my parents to hear him as we drive off.

Their heads turn toward one another, then back at the two of us.

"Happy to have you," Mom replies.

"You're always welcome," says Dad.

You've got to love my parents. They're troupers. Even when I say or do dumb things, they find a way to let go of their anger at me. With each other? Well, that's another story.

When we arrive at the house—big and white as expected— Jaz stares up in amazement as Mom, Dad, and I take the cobbled path to the front door.

"Wow, it looks like the White House!"

Sure, it's a big home with a lot of windows and trimmed bushes spread around the front. I don't see the big deal. Just another box that people live in. A box with beds and bathrooms. Why does all this extra furniture and property matter so much to adults?

Dad knocks three times. The double doors open to his newer friends, Soren and Rutna. They are wearing shiny, colorful saris and kurtas. They cheer and welcome my dad with big hugs, then they just peer over at us. "Thank you for coming to our anniversary party," they say. None of Dad's friends are ever overly kind to Mom. She taught herself Hindi and learned to cook the best egg curry in the world but it's never been enough. Always the outsider.

"Don't you have just one son?" asks Soren.

"This is Kamal's friend, Jaz."

Jaz bows like he's meeting a king and queen. "It's an honor to meet you, sir. You live in a palace."

Soren looks flattered. Not surprising. I would be too if I were getting my butt kissed.

"Please, come in. Make yourself at home. The boys are upstairs in Junior's room."

The grown-ups walk into the grand living room while Jaz and I make our way upstairs to their kid's room. I'm sure he's a spoiled brat like the other kids at the other parties. I'm not impressed. Anyone with money can buy expensive things. I bet he can't build a tent out of sticks!

We knock at the door that says "Soren" on it and where all the laughter and shouting is coming from. Then, when we open the door, it feels like we're entering a space station. Shiny gadgets crowd shelves. An enormous TV takes up most of the far wall, opposite a king size bed with a metallic colored blanket. Four kids our age are crowded in front of the mega screen, playing a video game. They don't even notice us standing in the doorway.

"Hey, guys." I announce myself. The zombies grunt and acknowledge our presence.

It takes another minute of being ignored before I decide to say more. "I'm Kamal. My dad Rishi is friends with Soren's dad. This is my friend, Jaz."

Suddenly, the game pauses and the boys rear their heads toward us.

I can't believe it.

Soren?

"Soren?" I say aloud. Soren, Soren. Bruppie Soren. Used-to-be-my-friend-but-is-now-a-jerk-Soren.

"Hey, loser," he says. "I've seen you with this F.O.B at school. Where you from, F.O.B?"

"How annoying. Your dad is friends with my dad now?" I say.

Jaz leans over to me and whispers. "What is this 'F.O.B.' I keep hearing?"

"It means fresh off the boat," I whisper back. "It's a mean way of saying you're an immigrant."

"Oh, okay," he says, then turns to the group. "I sure am!" Jaz says. "I am from Pakistan."

One of the kids spits out soda and starts to laugh hysterically. He runs to a corner to cough and catch his breath. Two of the kids follow him and leave Soren with us.

"You let a Paki into my house?" Soren says.

"What are you talking about?"

"Pakis aren't cool. They're terrorists." Soren stands up, his chest puffing outward. "Kamal, you better leave before I tell the adults that he tried to pull a knife on us."

"A knife? What knife?"

"This one." Soren walks over to the drawer in his bedside table and pulls out a Swiss army knife, and pushes the blade open with his thumb.

Jaz and I take a step backward.

"Whoa, where did you get that?" I panic.

"I stole it from The Sports Authority. But I'll tell them your friend brought it to the party and tried to use it on us."

We say nothing. What can we? We back out of Soren's room. And almost as quickly as it stopped, the banter and chatter and noise of a hundred video game zombies being struck down returns behind the closed door.

※ ※ ※

Jaz and I spend the next hour hanging out on

the dimly lit back patio, eating potato chips and chugging mango lassis. It's dark outside but the full moon in the sky is shining just bright enough so we can see each other's faces.

"Man, I can't believe those guys," I say out loud, again, after too many minutes of silence.

"Bullies are bullies no matter where you are in the world," responds Jaz. "The question is, how do we stand up against them? We cannot fight back. They are too big and too dangerous."

"Okay, so what do we do?"

He stands up and paces back and forth. He closes his eyes, searches deep inside his brain for a bright idea.

"Got it! They may be big. But we are smart. AND sneaky. . . We will put worms into their dinner."

"Huh? How are we going to do that?"

"Easy. Come with me."

Jaz grabs the near-empty chip bowl, dumps out the crumbs and runs across the grass to where there are no lawn lights. He gets down on his hands and knees, rolls up his sleeves, and starts digging into the dirt with his hands. I run after him.

"Do you have a flashlight?" he asks.

"My watch glows in the dark."

"Shine it on me, please."

I press the side button that lights up the watch's face in a green tone and turn my wrist upside down, focusing the glow on Jaz. He kneels up, holding fistfuls of mud with dozens of worms squiggling all about. He sticks them into the bowl, then grabs for more.

"Good thing it rained this morning," he declares. "The ground is gooey and moist. Worms are easy to find in wet dirt."

We run back inside and make our way toward the kitchen. Dinner hasn't been served yet and the caterers are still heating food. I feel nervous and excited at the same time. I've never done anything like this in my life. Jaz looks confident, like he's on a mission.

"Over there, the palak paneer." He points to the rectangular tray that a waiter has just taken out of the oven and placed on top of the stove. It's a spinach curry that kind of looks like mud already, brown and green, and slimy. It actually tastes delicious.

Once the waiter walks out of the room, we sneak over to the stove. I hold the bowl while Jaz tips the tray just enough to pour the curry in. Using a serving spoon from the counter, Jaz stirs the mixture and blends in the mud and worms. He combines it all so well I can barely tell they're in there.

We grab a few small bowls and spoons, place

them onto a serving tray, and sneak back upstairs. Fortunately, these types of houses always seem to have two staircases. One leading from the front of the house and another from the back. We take the back steps this time so no one will see us.

Jaz places the tray in front of Soren's door, knocks hard, and calls out loudly in a high-pitched voice: "Sweetheart! A snack for you and the boys!"

"Thanks, Mom!" Soren calls out.

We quickly race down the hall and into an empty room, out of sight, and stare through the sliver where the door is cracked open to see if they take our bait. We see Soren's door open and a pair of hands swipe the tray. Then, the door slams shut again.

We carefully tiptoe back and place our ears to the door. We hear the spoons dinging on the bowls. Then chewing. First, happy sounds. Yum. But then, one by one, moaning. One kid belts out a scream I'll never forget.

"AH!!! A WO-WO-WO-WO-WORM!!!!"

Jaz and I crack up, leaning on the door so hard that when it swings open we fall to the floor, crying out happy tears. The boys all bolt out, shoving past us, spitting and wiping at their tongues. They run to the bathroom to wash out their mouths.

We get to our feet and hurry downstairs to see dinner being served buffet style. We get in line just behind Mom and Dad.

"Why are you so filthy, Jaz?" Mom asks.

"We were playing outside!"

"Outside? Here?"

I'm not sure why but I thought by being downstairs, away from the chaos, I could ignore the consequences that were about to happen. But no. Before long, Soren and his buddies charge down the stairs, searching for us. Their cheeks are covered in the residue of curry and mud. Mom sees them, then glares back at us with wide concern.

"Oh, no. What did you do?"

Minutes later, on the drive home, Dad is dozing in the passenger seat while Mom is behind the wheel. She's quiet. The car is quiet. Only the occasional streetlamp brings a passing light in. Jaz and I are in the back seat, toothy grins clear in the darkness.

"How embarrassing," Mom says softly. "You're lucky your dad's friends weren't too upset."

"I'm sorry, Mom. But those guys were asking for it."

"I thought I taught you not to give into bullies. You're no better than them now."

"It was my fault," Jaz interrupts. "I am sorry, ma'am."

The rest of the drive home is silent. We pull into the supermarket parking lot and Jaz hops out.

"Thank you for a great evening!" he says, peering in through my window.

"I'm supposed to just leave you here?" says Mom. "It's so late. Where is your actual home?"

"Right behind the building, over there." Jaz points in the distance. Mom tries to follow his finger to the location. By the time she twists her head back, he is gone.

Mom just sits there in her seat and sighs.

"You're not going to like this. But I don't want you hanging around him again. Do you hear me?"

"Mom!"

"You haven't been acting like yourself since you met him."

"But. . . he's my friend."

"Kamal, I mean it."

I slump back into my seat and pout. I glare down at my shoes crusted with mud, and maybe even worm guts and curry. I can barely see through the darkness. So much darkness.

CHAPTER 7

A week goes by before I speak to Jaz again. I try my best to avoid him, though it isn't easy. I don't want to duck him. After all, he's the first kid in a long time who's made me feel worthwhile. Like I have a right to be me. I thought I was fine with being picked on and being a little afraid most of the time but he's shown me that I don't have to live that way. But I also don't want to betray Mom. So, I show up late to homeroom, a crowded class, and sit in the back behind the basketball players, who all achieved growth spurts way earlier than the rest of us. I eat my lunch sitting in the bathroom stall, aware that, as I eat my tinfoil protected sandwich, there is a moat of dirty toilet water right beneath the lid.

Then, only a few days before Halloween, Jaz corners me by my locker. I'm on my knees, putting my books away on the bottom shelf. It's not easy to get up and run when I'm not flat on my feet.

"Look, I know you are mad at me about getting you in trouble. But, please. You cannot stay mad forever."

I throw him a stony glare. I can't bolt but at least I can show how disappointed I am. He has no idea how mad I am. But not at him, really. I'm mad at how hard it all seems. Why can't it be easy? Why can't I be friends with whoever I want? And be silly? And, yeah, sometimes, get in trouble?

"Come on. It is Halloween!" He's whining and looks so sad now, like a puppy begging to play. "It will not be fun without you."

Truth is, my Halloween won't be fun without him. I usually trick-or-treat alone and only bother with a few houses on my block. I'm not exactly singled out or anything but I always seem to be near mischief; I'll accidentally stumble into a group of kids with cans of shaving cream, cartons of raw eggs, and rolls of toilet paper, who don't look like they're running a donation drive. In fact, they're looking to unload it all on houses and trees, and candy seekers like me. This year, I can have some backup from Jaz. And I'll finally get to celebrate the holiday, maybe even fill up my pillowcase with candy instead of just a few measly bits.

"Okay, fine," I tell him. "But I can't tell my folks we're hanging out. They're still a little upset."

"I understand." Jaz bows his head solemnly. Suddenly, he jerks back up quickly, another one of his ideas popping into his head. "We should go to the mall tomorrow. For costumes?"

I pause, think about it for a few seconds, then agree to the meetup. How much trouble could we possibly get into at the mall?

"Great!" he says gleefully. "I really am sorry about the party. I hope your parents will forgive me."

"Me, too," I say.

I'm halfway down the hall and he shouts after me. "Hey, Kam!" he says and smiles. "It was pretty funny though." He wriggles his fingers around in the air. As if they're worms.

"It was the best," I smile.

* * *

The next day, after school, I ride my bike the two and a half miles to The Square Mall, a small shopping mall with about a couple dozen stores that was built in the 1980s in the shape of a literal square. I can walk completely around its perimeter of stores in about ten minutes and never get lost. It can get old quickly but I still like walking around anyway and looking at things I don't need and can't afford — like those vibrating massage chairs in The Sharper Image.

Halloween-themed stores always pop up in droves around late August. They're only open for a few months, then vanish like ghosts a few days after October 31st. I lock my bike up near the entrance to one — Spooky Town — to meet Jaz near the front.

Spooky Town is like an amusement park inside: orange and purple streamers hanging from the ceiling, robotic lawn monsters popping out of the walls, the Addams Family theme song playing over the loudspeaker. The spirit of the holiday is alive and well inside of these ghoulish walls. Surrounded by the smell of plastic and nylon, I temporarily forget about lying to my mom about being here instead of the library. I forget that, even though I feel like I know him better than anyone, Jaz is still as masked to me as some of these costume dummies.

He's not where we said we'd meet by the front so I circle around to find him. He's already in the heart of the store, trying on a bunch of different masks, a giddy energy buzzing from him. I tap him on his shoulder. It looks like he's wearing a pumpkin on his head. When he turns around, I came face-to-face with President Bush — the current one, not his father.

"Ah!" I shriek, stumbling backwards.

"Weapons of mass destruction!" he exclaims, throwing his arms up in the air with excitement.

"Are you crazy? Take that thing off your head before you scare someone."

"Is that not what he always says on TV?"

"Who cares? You can't say that in public. You'll get in major trouble."

"But it is on sale."

"Come on. Take that thing off and let's find costumes we can both wear together. You know, like a team!"

Jaz pulls off the mask and tosses it back into the clearance bin, next to a pile of other faces. We walk around for a while, trying on different masks and wigs, chuckling and cracking jokes. We consider dressing as Harry Potter and Ron Weasley except the red wig doesn't look good on either one of us. Then, Jaz spots U.S. Army costumes: green and brown fatigue uniforms complete with toy automatic rifles. He dashes over to them.

"Whoa, these are so cool."

"Um, kinda? The real ones probably have a lot more gear and I'm pretty sure their guns don't have orange plastic tips at the ends of them."

"How about we go as troops?" he asks.

"Why? I thought we were looking for something magical or supernatural?"

"What is more super than soldiers? Mr. Wright told us he used to serve in the army. He will be so impressed with us if we walk into school on Halloween with these on."

"I thought you didn't care what anyone thinks?" I hate to think it and I'd never say it aloud, especially to Jaz, but no one would think it cool if he put this on right now. It would just make things worse.

"I just think he will be impressed is all. Plus, Tyler, Kevin, and Jimmy will not mess with us in these." He holds the outfit up to his neck, puffing it out with his chest.

Before I can argue more or think about agreeing, Jaz does that thing where he grabs my hand and dashes us on the next part of our adventure. We're at the cash register throwing down the last three years of my birthday money and a twenty he said his dad gave him specifically for the event. When he says it, I immediately realize it's not true.

With our purchases in hand, we head towards the exit. Before we make it to the door, Jaz reaches into his shopping bag and pulls out the toy gun that came with the costume. He points it toward a teenage girl working behind the counter of Sunglass Hut. "Stop right there, miss," he says to her, grinning.

The salesgirl raises her hands in the air in shock. An older woman in the distance screams in fear. Jaz looks around, unsure what all the excitement is about. I look at the gun and notice the orange plastic tip hasfallen off.

"Jaz, th-th-they think it's re-re-real!" I try to explain, tripping over my words. "Qu-quick, pu-put it aw-aw-away."

"What? How can they think that? I am just having fun."

"Put it away. Now!" I scream.

Just then, a mall security guard sprints in our direction. Jaz freezes, a cardboard cutout version of himself.

"Stop right there!" The security guard yells.

"Run, Jaz!" I loop my arm with his and drag him until he starts to move his own feet. We hurry through the exit, the guard about twenty steps behind us. Luckily, he's kind of old and slow.

Once we get to my bike, I unlock it quickly and hop onto my seat. "Get on," I tell Jaz. He puts his feet on the back pegs and swings his arms around my shoulders, clutching our shopping bags in his hands. I pedal as fast as I can till we lose sight of the parking lot. I am actually amazed at my speed.

By the time we reach a side road, about a half mile away, next to an overgrown, vacant parking lot, I stop to rest and catch my breath. Jaz jumps from the back of my bike.

"What happened back there?" he asks.

"They thought you had a real gun." I say, pointing and panting from exhaustion.

"Holy cow! But it has an orange thingy at the end of it! And. . . and I am just a kid. That is crazy."

"It fell off. It doesn't matter anyway. You pointed it at someone. You should never do that. Ever."

"I have seen other kids do things like that," he says. I've never seen him like this before. Worried now, blood drained from his face, his eyes squinting. He is confused, trying to piece together how one thing can be okay for some kids — the white ones, the rich ones. But not for him. This moment is the worst I've ever felt, I think. Knowing there is nothing I can say to make unfairness make sense.

So I say the only thing I can. "I know. . . But that doesn't make it okay."

"Oh, no, no, no. You think they are looking for us?"

"I don't know. Maybe."

"I cannot get in trouble with the government, Kamal!" Jaz starts breathing heavily, panicking now.

"The government? What are you talking about? It was a mall cop. He's not even a real one."

"We cannot ever go back there. Never again. My uncle will be so mad!"

"What uncle? Why are you freaking out?"

"Come on. We need to keep going. If they catch me, they will send me back."

"Who? Send you back where?"

"Karachi! The government! They will send me back to Pakistan!"

※ ※ ※

On the way home, I pedal slowly, so many thoughts racing through my head. My brain is knocking around my skull like a pinball.

By the time I walk through my door, it's pitch-black outside. My parents' cars are parked in the driveway, and I know they're going to be livid that I'm getting home after sunset. But I walk in the front door without any fight in me.

Mom's sitting at the kitchen table in front of two empty plates. I can hear the faint sound of the TV in the den where Dad usually goes at the end of the day.

My place at the table is still set, the food on my plate is untouched. As soon as she hears me, Mom outborrows; she's been bent over, forehead on the table, fists clutching at her hair.

"Where, Kamal, have you been?"

"I left you a note," I say.

"The library closed several hours ago. It's dark."

"I know. I went to the mall for a Halloween costume after. I'm sorry."

"Alone?"

"What do you mean?"

"Did you go with anyone?" she asks.

"No."

"Don't lie to me again, Kamal. I don't know what's happening to you. You never used to hide things from me."

I don't say anything. My skin is buzzing and my head is spinning, and I suddenly feel very hungry. Hungry and thirsty, and mad.

"Where's Dad? Is he mad, too? Or is he just drunk asleep on the couch?"

"Kamal!"

"Never mind," I explode. "I'm sorry I'm late. I just wanted to get a costume. But it doesn't matter anyway because I'm probably not going trick-or-treating. I'll just go to my room."

"Kamal, I saw you with Jaz."

"What do you mean? You were at the mall?"

She sighs and pushes her chair back, walks over to me. Even though I am short for my age, she is, too. And it doesn't take much effort to look into her eyes. They're not so mad now but sad. "I was picking up candy for the trick-or-treaters at Spooky Town and saw you two."

"You were spying on me?"

"I wasn't spying—"

"—and you didn't say anything? You just let us keep hanging out? Is it part of your plan to punish me?"

"Don't turn it around, Kamal. I specifically told you not to see that boy anymore. He's bad news."

"Says who? The president? The anchors on TV? Mall cops?"

"Please, Kamal. I'm just concerned."

"Well you know what, Mom? I'm concerned, too. About my friend. Because you were right. His family did come here illegally. And he was separated from his parents. And he's living with his uncle right now and using his name. He's scared. And he tries to hide how scared he really is by making other people feel good, by making other people laugh. Like me. Even you! He tried to make you laugh like a million times but you never did. You never did. And do you know how confusing this all is? You ever think about that? That he's my only friend?"

She's stone cold now; her mouth is a gaping hole. There's a burning lump in my throat and one in my belly. And suddenly, all at once, the tears just fall in torrents down my face.

"What do you mean? Did he tell you this? When did he tell you this?"

"Today. After the mall. His name isn't even Jaz. That's his uncle's name. He's living with him until his parents can come to him."

I can't breathe anymore. I'm still crying and before she can say another word, I pick up my chilly plate of food and stomp upstairs to my room. I've had enough of hiding and lying, of asking myself what is right and wrong. I don't know which way is up anymore, and I don't even care. My life has turned into a giant, slimy mud pie.

CHAPTER 8

✝※★

The next day is Halloween. The original plan was for Jaz and me to wear our costumes to school, since most kids go trick-or-treating right after the last bell rings. But now I'm not so sure. Not after the argument with mom last night. I'm mad at myself for cluing her into Jaz's secrets. But, deep down, I think I wanted her to know; I am hopeful that she'll get over her feeling down on Jaz. Maybe I can even convince my parents to help him somehow. Could they sponsor or adopt him or something? It's worth a shot. I just need to make sure he doesn't mess up again.

I wake up in the morning and see my half-eaten plate of food on my nightstand. The inside of my mouth feels sour and warm; I hadn't brushed my teeth before bed. Just stormed upstairs, ate a little, and went to sleep.

The Spooky Town bag is sitting on the floor. I take the army costume, wrapped in plastic, from the bag and hold it in my hand. I know it's going to be tight on me and my fat will bulge a little. I'm suddenly annoyed by the kid models posing on the package, the black girl and white boy, who look like they've been fitted by a tailor at Macy's.

I dress in the fake fatigues and it feels. . . not great. Not because it is tight but because it only reminds me of the trouble at the mall. I was surprised Jaz even wanted to move forward with our plan. But after he had spilled his guts and we both calmed down, after we were quiet for a long time, watching the cars rush past us, we realized that the large security officer guy wasn't actually going to catch us, and we both decided Halloween was still on. We wanted the Milky Ways and the cool night air and cruising on my bike around town with everyone else, and these were the costumes we had chosen after all. We weren't going back to the mall to get new ones. We had parted, still shaken up, but in agreement about what we were going to wear the next day.

Halloween is a good excuse to act wackier than usual. As long as we stay close together, I know Jaz can get through the day without pulling a prank or getting into a fight. I know we can have fun.

Yesterday, before we left each other, I made sure to tell Jaz to leave the toy gun at home. He promised me he wouldn't bring it. We're lucky nobody at the mall recognized us in the commotion. Even luckier that my spying mom hadn't hung around the mall long enough to see the craziness (she would have mentioned it to me when we talked; she would have flipped out and grounded me till 2024). But bringing a weapon to school — even if it is plastic — that's pretty much the worst thing Jaz could do.

The tragedy at Columbine was only a few short years ago. Then, the very worst day happened last year in September. I'm surprised we don't walk through a metal detector at school now, like I hear my cousins in the city do. We do practice safety drills in case a school shooting happens. Every few months the kids in each classroom huddle in a corner and stay silent while Principal Snyder runs the drill. I'm still unsure how this will protect us if anything were to actually happen; I know Tyler feels the same (he's said it aloud before, during our corner huddle, while shoving his armpit into my face). But we all go along with the drill because it breaks up the boredom in class.

I can't lie to myself though — 9/11 was a real-life nightmare, one of the scariest days of my life, and anything we can do to make us feel safer is probably a good idea. My dad thinks there is no such thing as safe now. He used to commute to Long Island City before he got laid off. He told me that, when the planes crashed into the World Trade Center, the clouds of smoke were so intense and so vast they drifted up and over the East River and into the street where he parked his car, and that it was suffocating. I remember being so worried he wouldn't come home that night. But he did. I waited by the front door for hours, shivering, till finally, I saw his car pull up into the driveway. He sat there for a solid minute before getting out. I'll never forget his face as he walked up to the house. His head tilted to one side, eyes squinting back tears, his breathing heavy and staggered. I jumped into his arms. Mom hugged us both and wept.

I wasn't sure why the terrorists blew the buildings up in the first place. And I'm still not sure. Were they mad at us? People don't just blow things up for the fun of it. Do they? It doesn't make sense. No good has come from it. My dad hasn't really smiled, I mean really smiled, since that day. He doesn't even attend his usual Saturday morning ceremonies at the temple. He just sits in front of the TV, beer in hand, when he's not out looking for work.

It's all I can think about as I wear this dumb costume and look into the mirror. There are people, a lot of people, real people, braver than me. Who have a lot more stories to share and who deserve to wear these clothes.

I hope Jaz doesn't bring the gun.

✳ ✳ ✳

Before I catch the bus, I try to psyche myself up. I run to the backyard and quickly rub dirt under my eyes. Like soldiers do in the movies. I catch the bus and take the ride to school. With every passing moment, my excitement for the day begins to balloon again. I just hope it doesn't pop.

Jaz is waiting by his locker for me. The outfit is baggy on his scrawny body. It's the first time I've seen him in clothes that look and smell new. He doesn't seem nervous or dwarfed at all though. You'd never know he was a mess only the afternoon before. "Aye, aye, Captain!" he says, as I walk up to him.

I don't see the plastic gun, so I play it cool, as if nothing did in fact happen the afternoon before, and that I know nothing about Jaz's real life or that I blabbed it all to my mom. Even still, I feel my heart beating fast and my palms sweating really bad.

"Um, I think that's what pirates say," I explain. "Not Army men. How about, 10-4, General?" I salute him. He does the same.

"We look pretty handsome," he says.

"Handsome? You think so?" The only time I am ever called that word is by Mom when I wear a suit for a wedding or another boring family event. I fake a smile and worry about spilling food all over my "good clothes" as she calls them. And then she calls me her "handsome boy."

"Yeah, Kam. Ladies love men in uniform."

"Says who?"

"Someone said it on *Cops*. They used to play it in Karachi."

I laugh. As we stand there, talking, Tyler walks by. He's dressed as a devil. Black cape, red horns, plastic pitchfork. He stops and stares at us, then begins laughing hysterically, slapping his thighs.

"What are you guys supposed to be?"

"Soldiers," I say.

"From where?" He continues cracking up, holding his belly.

"America!" Jaz says. I pull him by the sleeve as he tries to move toward Tyler.

"You two don't look like American soldiers."

"Oh, yeah?" I'm getting mad now, too. "What is an American soldier supposed to look like?"

Tyler pauses and thinks about it for a second. "You know, like Tom Cruise or Bruce Willis. Not like the. . ."

"The what?" I press him.

"The enemy!" he answers, motioning for the crowd that's now surrounding us to agree with him. We watch as some kids move on, others stay and either nod or shrug.

"You're an idiot, Tyler!" I regret it as soon as the words leave my lips. Tyler's face turns hot red and he takes two quick steps toward me now, his giant pitchfork pointing to my face.

Suddenly, Principal Snyder's voice projects over the loudspeaker:

"Excuse me, all students and faculty. We interrupt your morning for an important announcement. There's been an attack at the Halloween Day parade this morning in midtown Manhattan. There are no reports yet on any injuries or fatalities. No word on who is responsible for this tragedy. We will keep you posted with any further developments. Please proceed to your homeroom class and await more news. DO NOT leave the premises. We are securing the doors."

What follows is a blur. A burst of chatter fills the halls and kids scramble to class, looks of concern plastered on every face. Familiar fears and worry about parents and aunts and uncles and friends resurface and take command. Across the hall, one classroom door is wide open, and the teacher has the TV turned on to the local news station. The kids and teachers, who've yet to move on to their homerooms are cramming together to watch the live coverage. I hurry over and get on my tippy toes to see. On the screen, people in costumes are running from heaps of giant clouds of dirt and smoke. Some are lying on the ground, huffing for air, or in pain. Large block letters appear at the bottom of the screen: POSSIBLE TERRORIST ATTACK AT NYC HALLOWEEN PARADE. The view cuts to a news reporter with puffed up blonde hair and a streak of ash on her face. Everyone is starting to chatter again and I can hardly hear what's going on. But now, there's a picture within a picture; next to the reporter is a photo of a brown man, disheveled and dressed in a military T-shirt. POTENTIAL SUSPECT pops up under him. Even from a distance, some characteristics stand out. The long, angular face. The wide mouth. Bushy eyebrows.

"Whoa, that guy kind of looks like Jaz," Tyler says, loud enough for the entire classroom to hear.

"Take that back!" I say. I can feel steam coming from my ears. I leave my spot and, still on my tippy toes, get in Tyler's face. So close I can smell his breath and that stupid cologne he wears. I've never had the nerve to stand up to him like this.

"Jaz is more of an American than you'll ever be," I say.

"Oh, yeah?" Tyler says. His nostrils are flaring.

"Yeah! Right, Jaz? Jaz?"

I turn around to see Jaz bolting through the double doors at the end of the hallway. I try to chase after him but he is too quick and too far ahead. By the time I get through the doors, down the staircase, and through the exit, he is nowhere to be found.

I circle in place over and over, looking left and right. But it's no use. I wonder what else I can do. Who can I call? Who would care?

It doesn't take too long for the school security guard to find me and tell me to go back inside. "Go back in. Now. I'm locking up these doors."

* * *

Homeroom comes and goes. I sit alone at lunch. Meanwhile, we are all kept up to date on the events occurring downtown, less than an hour away from us, by the TV sets in each classroom that have all remained on, even if muted. After a few hours, word spreads that some have been hurt but none killed. The suspect is still at large.

I am happy to know everyone will survive.

But I definitely don't feel relieved.

CHAPTER 9

After school, I go straight home. I'm in no mood to go trick-or-treating. When I get off the bus, I see Grandma Clarita's car in the driveway. She usually visits on Halloween, something about it being Mom's favorite holiday when she was a kid and wanting to relive those memories with her, and with me. When I was younger, she'd walk with me around the block to collect candy from neighbors. As I got older, she found it more fun to hand out chocolate bars from our doorstep.

There'll be no memory making today. I'm in no mood to see her, especially today, especially after what she said a few weeks earlier about Tio Héctor and immigrants and Muslims.

Mom and Grandma are sitting in the den with the 24-hour cable news channel turned on high volume. A few people dressed in shiny suits are sitting in a circle, talking loudly, talking over each other. At the bottom of the screen: EXPERTS DISCUSS ONGOING THREAT OF TERRORISM: SHOULD THE U.S. BAN ALL IMMIGRATION?

"See, Kam? This is what I was talking about."

"Um. . .how about 'hello', Grandma?"

She doesn't answer me. Instead, she puts her arm around Mom. "They say the suspect is long gone. Still. . . This, baby, is scarier than any Halloween fright."

I scream. AAAAAAAHHHHHHH! I scream so loudly that I need to close my eyes and ball my fists to get it all out. So loudly that Mom and Grandma are shaken from their trance. They turn off the TV set and tell me to calm down.

"Calm down? How can you say that? There are good immigrants out there. Good Muslims. Like Jaz!"

"Who's Jaz?" Grandma asks.

"He's a new boy at school that Kamal has become friends with."

"You let him hang out with a Muslim kid?"

"I can't believe this. What is wrong with you guys?" I'm still fuming mad, my hands still balled up, my body knotted up like a pretzel.

"We're just looking out for you, Kamal," Mom says in her serious voice.

"Are you? Behind my grandma and mom, the two women I love most in the world, the two women who cook with me and tell me stories from their cultures, and tell me only to fight with my words, there is a wall of framed family photos. Smiling at Thanksgiving. Smiling at my cousins' apartment. Smiling on our camping trip last summer. I want to break every single one.

"I'm going trick-or-treating!" I tell them and stomp away.

✳ ✳ ✳

The next half-hour will go down as one of the loneliest times of my life. I walk down my street in a haze, door-to-door, and hold out my pillowcase as each one opens. A robotic journey. For a sad sack.

Some adults ask me "Trick or treat?" As if they actually want me to answer the question. All I can do is mumble just enough so they'll hand over the sugar.

I complete a dozen houses when I start to see shaving cream and toilet paper flying around in the distance, only a block away. I'm in no mood to run or to fight. I turn back toward home and figure I'll eat some chocolate in my backyard away from the warzone of bathroom products. If I can't hang with Jaz, at least I can hang in our fort.

When I open the side fence, I see rustling from the sheet that covers our fort. "Who's there?" I say in a loud but wimpy voice. "Come out now or you'll be sorry."

"It's me."

"Me who?"

"Jaz."

I walk closer and lift up the bottom of the sheet. He's sitting there, in the dirt, holding his knees together. His backpack is tucked behind him.

"What are you doing? How long have you been here?"

"I was scared. I didn't want to go home." He's still wearing his Army pants but he's in a big, white Nike shirt now. There's snot running from his nose and his eyes are red. He's been crying.

"So, you've been here all day?"

He nods, shivers a little. I plop down on the ground next to him.

"You know, I don't think you're a terrorist. You know that, right?" I say, trying to comfort him. "This isn't about you. Everyone is just freaked out about what happened."

"Yes. But they will look into it. Once they find out

I am not a citizen, they will deport me... or worse."

"Who says 'they'll' find out?"

"They are bound to find out."

"Well, you can't hide forever. You can't live under sticks and a bedsheet your whole life. You'll get too big for this tent."

"Can I sleep here? Just tonight?"

I can see the back of my house a few yards away and wonder what I should do. If I go inside to tell Mom and Grandma that my illegal-Muslim-immigrant-fugitive friend is hanging in our backyard, they'll probably call the cops and I'll never see him again. I'll probably be locked in my room till I turn eighteen or maybe even be sent to juvenile detention for being an accomplice.

"Here. Eat something." I reach into my pillowcase and pull out some candy bars. He starts unwrapping and devouring them, one by one.

"Thank you." He smiles, his mouth covered in chocolate.

"I'll sneak you some real food and a blanket in a little while."

"I am sorry, Kamal."

"It's okay. We'll figure it out."

As I crawl out, Jaz lies down on his side, using his backpack as a pillow, and stares out through the sliver of the sheet. I can only see his deep brown eyes, the shadows underneath. They're fixed on the dimming sunset behind me, beyond the top of the trees. It's the most unsure I've ever seen him. What's he thinking about, I wonder. His parents? His future? I feel so much for him. My life has been safe up until this point. His hasn't at all. I have a duty to protect my friend. I can't let him down.

"Hey, Kam?"

"Yeah?" I whisper.

"You are like a brother to me. Good night."

I want to cry. I never had a brother but always wanted one.

CHAPTER 10

I creep back inside the house. Mom and Grandma are still watching the stupid news like a couple of zombies. They don't even know I've come back. I reach into the linen closet and pull out an old quilt, quietly open the fridge and grab the nearest Tupperware of leftovers for Jaz. I sneak back outside. He's already asleep, cradling his backpack. I cover him with the quilt, leave the food nearby, and head back in and up to my room for the night. Wondering what the next day will bring us, and the ones after that.

I can't sleep most of the night. I toss and turn, and wonder how Jaz is doing out there, alone, under a roof made of tree branches. It's not too cold but I should have snuck him upstairs and let him sleep in my closet or on the floor or something. I could have thrown my stuffed animals over him, the ones no one is supposed to know I have. But he can.

The next morning, still in my pajamas, I throw on my bomber jacket and tiptoe downstairs. Nobody in the house is awake yet, so I'm extra careful as I take each step into the kitchen. I pour orange juice into a paper cup and butter a piece of toast, and then, gently, I open the back door to go check on Jaz.

"Good morning," I say only a few steps from the fort. "You thirsty?"

No answer.

I move closer. The tent is completely silent. The only sound is the bedsheet rustling in the strong morning gust.

Finally, I peek inside. He's gone. Just a quilt, a candy wrapper, and his backpack remain. I wonder if he is walking around the backyard, maybe using nature's bathroom? No sign of him anywhere. Could he have headed back to his uncle's? It's Saturday after all. He doesn't have to show up to school and face his fate just yet.

Without going back inside, I walk my bike out from the side yard and into the street. I chug the paper cup of juice, crumble it up, and put it in my jacket pocket. I stick the toast between my teeth and push off. I pedal and chew, pedal and chew. I don't know exactly where Jaz's uncle lives but I remember he mentioned the Mayfair apartments behind the King Kullen.

When I arrive at the supermarket's parking lot, the breezy fall morning continues and pushes dead, red and yellow leaves around in all directions. The sky is now blue with fluffy, white clouds gliding by. I cruise around the property till I make it to the back-end, near the dumpsters. There's a rundown apartment complex sitting behind the lot, separated by a rusted, old chain link fence and some overgrown bushes. There's a broken opening in the fencing and a dirt footpath that leads from the other side of the fence — the apartments, my answer — to where I sit on my bike. I plan my next move. I'll hide my bike behind the dumpster and sneak in quickly. I consider rubbing dirt streaks under my eyes again. I'll be fast like a ninja, like a cat! But before I can do any of that, as I still sit on my bike, a brown man with graying hair appears from the hole in the fence, squeezing and contorting his body through the damaged metal wire.

"Excuse me." I wave to the man. I keep my distance, aware of stranger danger.

"Yeah?" he says.

"Do you know a boy who lives in there?" I point to the apartments over his shoulder.

"A boy?"

"Jaz Rafiq."

He bows his head and thinks for a few seconds. "No," he says. Then, he stares at me, hard, his brows raised. "Why do you ask?"

"He's my friend. He's my age, around my height. A long face, really skinny—"

"Mr. Rafiq lives alone and does not entertain visitors."

"So, there is a grown up with that name there, then?"

The man glares at me longer this time, his eyes lasers.

"He has gone and will not be returning for a long time. I suggest you leave."

What does that mean?

"Leave now, young man." His voice becomes angrier.

"But, but, but. . ."

I try to get out more words but I can't do it fast enough. He walks past me, expecting his word to be final. "I better not catch you over there," he calls over his shoulder. He grows farther and farther away, and once again I am alone with only my bike and the dirt path.

I could turn away now. I should turn away.

CHAPTER 11

Okay, okay. I know I'm only a kid and I'm always supposed to do as adults say but this is a special situation. My friend's life could be in danger. I need to make sure he's safe, or at least find some clues that can lead me to him.

I make sure the old man is completely out of sight. Then, I carefully place my bike in between some overgrown shrubs sitting against one part of the broken fencing, and cover it with recently fallen, damp leaves so no one will see it. Crouching down, I look out for anyone coming or going in the apartment complex. The coast is clear, so I creep slowly through the hole, and onto the footpath. Behind me is the wobbly fencing that faces the parking lot. Ahead, wild, untamed foliage. I feel like I'm entering a mystic passageway to ancient ruins.

Once I finally get to the end of the path, I can fully see the group of three-story-high red brick buildings. They look abandoned, forgotten. Overgrown grass and weeds stand tall and nearly reach the height of the first-floor windows. The whole place is eerie, as if nobody has lived here for decades. I wade through the grass like a soldier creeping on enemy territory in search of his fellow troops, like I'm in *Saving Private Ryan*. I saw it at the multiplex with Dad; he never tells Mom when he takes me to see R-rated movies.

I sneak up to a window that is only half-way covered by blinds, and crouch directly underneath. I'm not sure what I think I'll see. Jaz tied to a chair and the CIA questioning him? My mind is racing. I gulp back phlegm and acid rises in my throat. I lift my head, inch by inch, my fingertips gripping at the paneling.

Finally, I can see inside. No men in suits or any signs of Jaz. Instead, there's a tiny, old, brown-skinned woman wrapped in a blanket, a hijab covering her head. She's swaying back and forth in a wooden rocking chair. She's holding a lit candle between her palms. Sitting on the floor next to her is a little girl coloring a single piece of paper with a bright red crayon. There are no lights on, just the candle's flame and a little bit of sunlight peeking through the blinds. The room looks messy, clothes scattered all over the floor and covering the seat cushions of a nearby couch. Why are they living this way? I focus on the girl, red crayon in hand. She looks to be filling in the roof of a house. Her scene is nearly complete.

Near her, on the beige carpet, there's a shadow that's caught her attention. She puts down the crayon and hovers over to get a closer look. Oh no! It's mine. I freeze in place. But the damage is done and she rears her head in my direction.

"Yanzur!" The little girl yells out. The old lady sits up and follows her finger, which is now pointing directly at me.

I duck quickly to the ground. I don't run immediately. I'm not sure what to do.

I hear a door open, only a few feet away from where I'm kneeling. The elderly woman steps out, waddling her way toward me, speaking softly in a language I've never heard. I stand up and face her, still stiff. She doesn't look upset but I can tell from her tone that she's trying to ask me a question. She hands the candle to the little girl, who takes it happily with two hands.

"I'm looking for my friend," I say, knowing she probably won't understand me. I have to try. She continues saying words I don't recognize. The palms of her hands are now facing the sky, her shoulders shrug. She looks just as confused as me.

"Jaz. Jaz Rafiq," I tell her. "Do you know Jaz Rafiq?"

"Jaz?" She flips her hand over and lowers it to the height of my head, as if she's measuring how tall I am. "Wulid, wulid."she repeats, pointing at me with her other hand.

"Jaz. Me. Yes, me. A boy like me." I pat my chest.

She tilts her head and then points upwards.

"Up there?" I ask.

She nods. "Wulid jayid," she says and points more clearly to the second floor. She puts up two fingers.

I smile and bow my head to thank her. She wrinkles her lips and forehead, a mixture of kindness and worry. Then, she backs herself and the little girl into her apartment, and quickly shuts the door.

Without hesitation, I creep to the end of the building, towards the stairway, and quietly tiptoe up the concrete steps. It's already cold outside but the building has a more intense iciness to it, like a cave or the back of the refrigerator when I'm reaching for leftover Kofta balls that Dad tries to hide in the back.

The second floor looks emptier than the first. Mold and moss are forming on the doors and windowpanes. I make it down the hall to the last apartment in the row, the one that sits directly above the old lady and little girl. This must be Jaz's home, the one she was pointing to. Holding onto the wall to position myself steady, I peek through the door jam. The room is dark.

With one knuckle, I softly tap on the door.

No response.

I try the doorknob but it's locked.

Just then, a voice yells from down the hall.

"Hey, you! Young man! What did I tell you?!"

It's the old guy with the beard. He looks furious. I panic and quickly reach for the door to another stair entrance behind me. I glide swiftly down the stairs. He's waiting for me on the last step, ready to catch me in his arms. I've run from enough bullies to know how to fake them out — instead of stampeding down the steps, I pretend to go left, then pivot right at the last second. It works. He catches a bundle of air and stumbles forward, using the stairs to break his fall.

I dash through the tall grass, down the narrow dirt path, and through the hole. I grab my bike from its hiding place. A few thorns prick me but I ignore the pain and jump on my seat. I pedal as hard as I can toward home and don't look back.

I'm no Tom Hanks. No Vin Diesel.

CHAPTER 12

I rush home, hop off my bike, and abandon it on the front lawn. I nearly trip over myself as I run to the backyard to check the fort once more. Still no Jaz. I crawl inside and plop down on the dirt, sweaty and exhausted, scratches all over my arms from the prickly bushes I ran straight through on my way back to the fence. I'm more confused than ever. I went searching for an answer and came back with more questions.

Jaz's backpack is still where it was left. I reach over, unzip it, and begin to rummage through its pockets. Maybe he left clues inside between the pages of his textbooks or slipped into the pockets of his

Trapper Keeper. I flip through everything. Nothing inside sticks out.

Then, in the final pages of his marble notebook, I find dozens and dozens of doodles and sketches. The pictures are of us, of our adventures together. He's drawn our friendship. We're superheroes of our own comic book. There's a series of panels, one of us eating Mom's leftovers at the lunch table, one of us playing tic-tac-toe at our desks before the bell rings, another constructing the campsite I am now sitting in. And so many more. I'm honored he did this. I had no idea he could draw. And he's talented, too. I can see this as a real book in a bookstore: **THE ADVENTURES OF KAMAL & JAZ**. That's the kind of book I'd read.

"Kamal, are you back there?" Mom shouts from the kitchen window, interrupting my daydream.

"Yeah, I'm here." I stay put, holding Jaz's notebook against my knees, remembering all the memories we made together. I start to cry and I burrow my face into the pages. I'm sad. For my friend, that I lost him. For the simple, American life he'll never have. Simple. Is anyone's, really? It seems they're all mixed up. Like when you stuff a blender with all sorts of random food you find in the fridge, then hit the smoothie option. It pours out in a sort of brownish, greenish, pinkish foamy... blob. That's me — that's us.

"What are you doing under there?" She's come down to check on me now. She kneels down and looks inside so I can only see her head, neck missing. "Are you crying? What's the matter?"

I show her Jaz's drawings. "He made these. Of us."

"He did?" She crawls the rest of the way in, takes the notebook from me, and carefully flips through the pages. I point to the characters and the speech balloons, and give the cliff notes of our adventures.

"Look, Mom, that's us. He drew us."

"Wow, these are great." I can tell she is impressed. She spends at least a few seconds on each page, tracing her finger over our faces.

"Did he give this to you?"

"No. He's gone, Mom. He ran away from school yesterday. After we found out about the attack. I found him here when I got home. He camped out here last night. Then, I came to check on him this morning and he was gone. He left this behind."

"Why did he run away?"

I had already told her most of the truth a couple nights before. But not all of it. Not about the mall scare or the doomed apartment complex. Or the bullying at school. Or the comparisons to the Halloween parade terrorist. And how he ran away right there and then.

How he didn't have a shot at having a good life here. Not really. But I will tell her now. It spills from me in one long, overwhelmed run-on sentence. And Mom just listens the entire time, her mouth in a flat line, her hand on my knee. When I finish, surprisingly, she doesn't scream at me or break down in tears. She just pulls me close and hugs me as hard as she can.

Then, she says something I truly didn't expect:

"Oh, Kammy. I'm so sorry. Perhaps we judged him too quickly."

"You are?"

"He shouldn't have to face all of that alone. He's just a boy."

"Where do you think he went?"

"I don't know but we need to tell someone. I think I should call the police."

"You can't!"

"But how else can we help him if we don't tell someone?"

"They'll send him back to Pakistan," I beg. "He'll get taken by terrorists! And I'll get in deep trouble for lying to the government!"

"Huh? Where do you hear these things?" Mom squints at me, grabs her chin.

"On the news," I say. "You have it on all the time."

Her cheeks turn reddish pink. She starts to stroke my knee. "You know. . ." she starts. ". . .your father almost didn't become an American citizen."

"Wait, really?" Did I hear her wrong?

"It's true. We married just after college. The student visa for his scholarship was weeks from running out and he was still searching for a job. We'd only just started seeing each other at the time but I knew I couldn't let him go back to India. He came from a poor family in a small village and he wouldn't have the same opportunities there as he did here. So, we got married at City Hall before it was too late. It didn't automatically make him a citizen. But it bought him time. Not too long after, he found a really great job. A couple of years later, we had you."

"You married Dad just to keep him in the United States?"

"No, I married your Dad because it made sense in my heart. It also happened to give him a chance at building a life he wanted. One we both wanted. One we could build together. Everyone deserves that chance, whether they've come here to make a better life or escape a bad one. That's what this country is all about."

"Did you love each other?"

"Of course."

"Do you still?"

"We loved each other then. And we love each other now. Marriage is just a tough thing after years and years of it. It's a work-in-progress. There are layers." She points to Jaz's art. "Like a drawing."

I look down again at the notebook spread out across both of our laps.

"Loving someone isn't easy, Kam. You can love them completely without understanding them completely. You accept the good and the bad. You don't give up on someone if you care about them. You care about your friend, right?"

"I do, I do. But Jaz doesn't have a student visa... and I can't marry him!" Mom laughs a little. I haven't seen her do that in a long time.

"It doesn't matter how he got here. The fact is, he's here now. We can't turn our backs on him."

She's right and I'm feeling less scared about the whole situation.

"So, on Monday morning, we'll go to your principal's office and tell her the whole story. Hopefully, we can all put our heads together and do something to help Jaz."

"But what if I get in trouble?"

"Don't worry. I won't let that happen, Kammy."

"I just hope I hear from him before then," I say.

"I'm sure you will," says Mom.

Grandma Clarita calls for us. I can smell her legendary scrambled eggs and mole pinto beans drifting out from the kitchen window. Mom and I go back inside, and I take a seat next to Dad. He's chugging his first cup of coffee; he looks like he needs it.

"Dad."

He slurps, sighs, and stares at me. So much love in those sleepy eyes. "Yeah, Kam?"

"Cut down on the beers, will ya? Mom doesn't like it when you drink too much."

His eyes widen still, then he glances over to Mom and Grandma standing by the stove. They both give him a smirk.

"And don't worry. Things will get better for you." I put my hand on his. "For us."

"Thanks, Kam," he says and takes another long gulp from his mug. He squeezes my hand tight.

Mom walks over to me and puts her hand on my shoulder.

"Thanks. You're a good dad," I tell him.

He bows his head and smiles, rests his hand over Mom's. She's just sat beside him.

Grandma tosses four drink coasters to the center of the kitchen table and places a sizzling pan on top. She takes a wooden spatula and serves a helping of eggs and mole pinto beans to each of us. I douse my plate with hot sauce, then pass the bottle to Dad. I love a lot of spiciness, just like he does.

CHAPTER 13

On Monday morning Mom drives me to school just like she said she would. After a long weekend plus a lot of thinking, I've decided confessing to Principal Snyder may be a good thing after all. Maybe she can help Jaz in ways I can't. Like, she can make phone calls to important people who'll get him out of this mess. I'm nervous about speaking to her. I spent most of yesterday playing the meeting out in my mind, how I'll present it. It's not like getting called on to read a piece of text aloud in Mr. Wright's class, all the historical events nicely organized and written out on a piece of paper.

We walk through the school's main entrance just as my normal bus pulls up to drop my neighbors off. The school flag outside the front door is at half-mast. The janitor usually adjusts it that way after a tragedy.

We sit and wait in the lobby of the front office. Five minutes feels like an eternity.

"Mom, I have to run to my locker."

"Now? But we're about to see Principal Snyder."

"I left one of my notebooks in there and I need it for class later. I won't have time to run back and get it after our meeting."

"Go get it and hurry back."

I wander down the hall, hoping to bump into Jaz. I even take the long way to pass by his locker, thinking he may be there like he was any other day. But the halls are completely empty. When I get to my locker, I notice the tip of a folded piece of loose-leaf paper sticking out of its vent. I undo the lock and open the door. The paper square drops to the ground. I grab it and quickly unfold the square. There are a few sentences in Jaz's handwriting, then a drawing underneath.

Kamal,

I am sorry I ran away. I had to go. Do not worry. I am safe with my uncle.

We will see each other again soon. Some day. I promise. I will write.

Take care of our fort.

Thank you for being my friend.

Love,

Jaz

Below the note, he's sketched the two of us sitting in our tent. We are smiling, our arms around one another. We look happy.

When I get back to the front office, Mom is still sitting in the row of seats outside of the principal's office door. I sit next to her and show her Jaz's note.

She studies it, then grabs my hand.

"Say whatever you have to say in there," she says softly.

Principal Snyder opens her door. "Come in, come in. Thanks for waiting."

We enter her office and slowly ease ourselves down into the two chairs facing her large wooden desk.

"So, Mr. Rao. Your mother told Mrs. Mayer at the front desk that you wanted to talk about Mr. Rafiq?"

I glance over at Mom. She doesn't move. Her eyes

just drift over to mine and blink a few times, as if to say, "The mic is yours."

Before I can say a word, Principal Snyder continues, "As you know, Mr. Rafiq left abruptly on Friday morning, just after the Halloween parade attacks occurred. We tried calling his home, but the phone was disconnected. We can't seem to get in touch with him or his family. Do you have any information regarding his disappearance? Where he went or why he ran off? We're very concerned."

I think about it for almost an entire minute. I cough, clear my throat, and scratch my head multiple times. What do I do? Will she help Jaz or make things worse? She's the reason he and I even met; she welcomed him into the school. The second I tell her what I know, will she insist on a fugitive manhunt? Will it even matter? I'm making myself dizzy.

"Um. No, I do not," I say. "I don't know where he is."

"Do you have anything to tell or show us that might help us find him?"

"I don't."

Principal Snyder looks to Mom for some adult assistance, but Mom just shrugs.

"I'm sorry that we wasted your time. We were hoping you would know more. He's just really worried about his friend," Mom says.

But Principal Snyder ignores Mom. Instead, she gets up and leans over her desk so she can look me right in the eye. "Kamal, if you have something you're not telling us, it's vital you do. You may be putting Jaz's life and your own life at risk."

"What is that supposed to mean?" Mom says.

"Well, Friday's events have left us all a little rattled, right? I'm hoping it's just a coincidence that one of my students ran off as soon as we all learned about the attacks. . . and well, the origins of the suspected wrongdoer."

"You mean one of your foreign students?" Mom insists.

"Look, we're all a little on edge. Please just let us know if you do end up hearing anything, okay?" With that, Principal Snyder gives one swipe at the crease on her skirt and walks out of her own office, leaving us in our chairs. Though she looks calm, I can tell Mom is shaking inside.

"I'm sorry." I'm not sure what else to say.

"That's alright, Kam." She puts her hand on my shoulder. "We'll talk about it at home. I've got to go to work now." She leans over and kisses me on my forehead, then whispers in my ear, "I'm proud of you."

※ ※ ※

I've suffered before from ignoring that age-old advice to never look down while you walk. I've tripped, bumped into doors, fallen into things. But I can't help but stare at Jaz's note as I walk to homeroom. I reread it over and over only looking up every now and then. Eventually, I do bump into something. And as luck would have it, it's Tyler's shoulder.

I brace myself. But he doesn't look mad. Actually, he looks happy to see me. Well, not happy-happy, but more relieved.

"I'm glad I bumped into you," he says.

"You are?"

"Yeah, I. . .I. . .wanted to see how Jaz is doing."

"Why?" I ask.

"I feel kinda bad about the things I said. About the terrorist stuff and all. I heard he ran away. Is that true?"

"Yes."

"Well, where is he?"

"In a better place, I hope."

"Huh? He's not dead, is he?"

"No," I assure him. "I'm just not sure he's coming back."

"Oh."

We both stand there for a few seconds shuffling our feet, not sure what to say next. Then, I just blurt out what I've wanted to tell him and his friends for a long time.

"You don't have to be such a jerk all the time, you know."

"Excuse me?"

"People like Jaz and me, you treat us like we're nothing. But we're not."

"Says who?"

"Says me. You, Kevin, and Jimmy have always made me feel small."

"You? Small?" There's his laugh. That smug cackle I've come to know so well.

"See, exactly! You put me down 'cause I don't look like you guys or act like you guys and because my family isn't like yours. But guess what? I like myself."

Tyler puts his hands in his pockets and shrugs his shoulders. For the first time, he isn't staring me down. "Okay. Okay. Fine. I guess I can give it a rest."

"Really?"

"Yeah," he says. And I swear, even though he doesn't show any teeth and even though his lips barely move, I swear I can see a little smile curl on his face.

"Sometimes!" he adds. Then, he barrels past me and turns the corner.

CHAPTER 14

On the bus ride after school, I daydream of the nap I'll take when I get home. I don't usually need extra sleep. But today, I feel more tired than usual. My brain and body feel worn out, as if I've just run fifty miles and taken a hundred math tests all at once — that kind of feeling.

Grandma Clarita's car is still in the driveway. I'm still in no mood to see her, pretty much stayed in my room all Sunday so I wouldn't have to. I keep hearing her words in my head. My sweet grandma saying such hurtful, ugly things. It hurts so much, lingers like a wasp sting.

Instead of raiding the fridge, I head straight upstairs to my bedroom, close the door behind me, and throw myself on the bed. I fall asleep quickly, still in my shoes and on top of the sheets. I guess experiencing tough stuff will do this to a person. Almost every night, whenever Dad gets home from work, he complains how tired he is. Mom, too. Living seems to make us all tired.

I wake a couple hours later to the smell of one of my favorite dishes: chana masala (chickpea curry—it's an Indian thing), burnt yellow rice with pigeon peas inside (arroz con gandules—it's a Puerto Rican thing), and meatballs (it's an Italian, well, Grandma Clarita's thing). That combination can only mean one thing: my grandma is cooking. She only learned to make one Indian recipe from my mom, who learned it from Dad's mom when she visited our country a few years back. She likes cooking it with her own type of rice plus those meatballs that earned her acceptance all those years ago. I love the mixture of flavors, especially when I add hot sauce all over it.

I'm hungry but hesitate to run downstairs since I'm still upset with her. Still, I figure maybe I can slip into the kitchen when she goes to read her magazines on the porch like she always does, and I'll make a plate to bring back to my room. Outside of my window, the sun is starting to go down. She likes sunsets.

I make my way slowly down the staircase and toward the kitchen. I can see she isn't in there. Three pots are sitting on top of the stove, steam rising from them. I delicately grab the wooden spoon sitting on the counter and dip it into the curry. I taste the edge of the spoon. It's so delicious, like always. Simmered to perfection.

"What are you doing, Kammy?"

Grandma is standing directly behind me with her hands on her waist. I didn't hear her enter the kitchen.

"Um, nothing." It's a lame response but I can't come up with anything better quickly. I try to act like nothing's bothering me but she knows. Grandmas always sense these things.

"Why don't you sit down and eat dinner like a normal child?"

"What does 'normal' even mean, Grandma?"

"I don't mean it that way, baby. Please, take a seat. I'll make you a plate."

I sit at the kitchen table while Grandma generously scoops rice onto a clean dish. Then, using a ladle, she smothers the rice with chickpea curry. She adds two meatballs and places the plate in front of me along with a big soup spoon (she knows how much I can't stand little spoons. I like to take big bites). The three smells embrace me like a hug, and I take a whiff.

"Mmmmmm," I sigh. "Why did you make this tonight?"

"It's your favorite."

"Oh," I say. I remember I'm mad at her and start to eat, avoiding her face.

"Kamal, I am so sorry for what I said. You are the best thing in our lives. In my life."

I tear up a little but I am also still eating. The salty tears seep into my mouth and mix with the curry. Ugh. My grandma has this sort of effect on me. There's something powerful about her and nearly every word she speaks makes me feel so much inside, whether good or bad.

She sits in the chair next to me. "Listen, baby. Your Mom's filled me in on what's happened since Halloween. Including in the principal's office this morning. I'm sorry I said some of those hurtful things about your friend. And I shouldn't have been so nasty towards your great uncle Héctor. Getting older doesn't necessarily mean you know more about the world. I'm still learning, just like you are."

Did I mention Grandma Clarita is the best apologizer ever? Yep, my heart just turned from a cricket ball to mashed plantains.

"Listen here, I'll tell you something I've never told anyone before. Not even your mom." She leans in.

"What?" I wipe tears from my eyes and sit up straight, waiting to hear what she has to say.

She takes a deep breath and pauses.

"Well, you see, my father wasn't technically an American citizen when we first arrived in New York all those decades ago. Puerto Rico had become a territory of the U.S. and the idea of property and citizenship were confusing for many years after that."

"A territory?"

"Yes, like when a country owns land but that land is not really part of the country."

"I don't get it."

"Well, your great grandfather was a proud man. He loved his home but there wasn't enough work in San Juan. We were very poor. So, he left when I was only a baby to come to work in New York. He was a great cook at home and used his talent to get a job working at a restaurant on the Lower East Side so he could send money home to us every month. A year later, when there was finally enough savings for us to come over from Puerto Rico, your great-grandmother and I came by airplane and were instantly granted citizenship."

"What about him?"

"He never came by plane or through Ellis Island. We never learned how he got here. He didn't meet us at the airport when we arrived. He had mailed us a letter with an address of where he was living, in a tenement, upstairs from his job. So that's where we went."

"When did he finally become a citizen?"

"He didn't, baby. By the time a year had passed, he was too afraid to tell the government. The restaurant allowed him to keep working there but they paid him in cash. It was different in those days. My mother, on the other hand, had to take a job making clothes in the Garment District. Meanwhile, they continued having babies."

"And then?" I ask her.

"And then... life went on," she says.

We stay seated for a long time and Grandma continues to tell me stories of her parents, of her family. After dinner, we eat Oreo cookies, twisting the wafers off and starting with the cream. Then, we clean up, wash the dishes, and put the leftovers in the fridge. I realize that Mom and Dad haven't come home and it's pretty late.

"How come nobody is home yet?" I ask. I probably should have asked her an hour earlier, but I was caught up in her stories, and my dinner.

"Your parents have gone out to eat. They needed a night out together. I told them I'd stay here an extra day and look after you this evening."

It's nice to know they're spending time with each other. They deserve a night out to have fun, away from their stress and from me.

Grandma and I head to the living room and watch a few reruns of *I Love Lucy*, our favorite show to watch together. Ricky Ricardo is my favorite TV character. I think I kind of look like him. Or maybe I just wish I do. He seems like he must have been so cool and so charming, like how I hope to be when I grow older. The credits are rolling when Mom and Dad walk in. They're holding hands, chattering excitedly.

"What's the matter, Celia?"

"Turn on the news." Dad says.

Grandma turns to the 24-hour news channel. EXCLUSIVE FOOTAGE OF HALLOWEEN PARADE ATTACK.

"The suspect appears to now be a white male, mid-30s, 5-11, a one John Hewitt, still at large," the news anchor says. "A motive is still being determined."

"We heard it on the radio as we were driving home from dinner," Mom says.

I want to be excited about this news. I want to shout out loud, to my parents, to Grandma: "See! See! The attacker isn't like Jaz at all!" Instead, I just miss him. And I know even if I say out loud that Jaz doesn't have a reason to feel scared, it doesn't mean it's true. It won't bring him back.

Life goes on.

* * *

I run out to the backyard with a flashlight while my family continues to watch the news. I return to the fort and Jaz's backpack, something I've yet to move. I flip to the back of his notebook – the one with the drawings. Maybe there's something I've missed. Page after page, I examine the pictures he's drawn. Finally, on the very last page, I see his final comic strip. There's a drawing of a bus. The head of a little boy — Jaz? —is peeking out through one of its windows. The bus rides along a winding road with twists and turns, getting smaller as it reaches the top right-hand corner of the page. The road ends at a highway sign that says DEARBORN. I've heard of that city before. Michigan. A big Muslim population.

I smile and breathe in the night air. The note Jaz left in my locker is still in my jeans pocket. I slip it between two pages of the notebook and hold it close to me.

Dearborn.

Could Jaz and his uncle be heading there?

Are his parents waiting for him? Will they be reunited?

Dearborn... Dearborn...

Do they have good places for friends to camp out there?

ACKNOWLEDGEMENTS

* † ※ ★ *

Bringing this book into the world has been an adventure. I'm grateful to many, many people for whom, without their support, this story wouldn't live.

Michelle, my wife and best friend. You're the best human I know. Your spirit, strength, and brilliance inspire me every day. Thanks for not letting me give up on myself and for showing me that I can be proud of who and what I am without fear or sacrifice. I am a better person because of you.

My mother Loretta, father Roop, and brother Ravi. You three are my core. I live to make you proud and feel seen in this crazy, mixed-up world. We have a place at the table now. And because of our journey, others will too. Thank you for always loving me and giving me the support I need to be something in this society. I am who I am because of you all.

My grandmother Elsie. I miss you every day. I miss your hugs, our handholding, your scalp massages as I laid on your lap while we watched old movies together, your cooking, your humor, your kindness, your toughness, your beauty, your presence. You are the greatest, Nani.

Thank you to Ujas Shah (the real Jaz), my best friend since Kindergarten, and his beautiful family, Rikita Shah and their beautiful child, Arjun Ujas Shah. When you're old enough to read this book, I hope you'll discover how ridiculous your father was (and still is). Of course, Jaz is only a caricature based on the real person, but his heart, silliness, and spunkiness are all true. You're my brother, Ujas.

Thank you to the entire Paw Prints Publishing/Baker & Taylor team. Amandeep Kochar, thank you for giving me and other authors the opportunity to have a voice. Your leadership, positivity, and kindness are unmatched. And thank you to Jagdeep Kochar and the Kochar family. Bobbie Bensur, thank you for your incredible direction and editorial brilliance. You're a born leader. This book wouldn't shine as brightly without you. You get me, you see me, your belief is invaluable. I'm so proud to have gone on this journey with you. Saanya Kanwar, thank you for editorial talent and insight. Your support has meant a lot to this project. Thank you to Daniela Alarcon for creating a book cover so beautiful that it brought me to tears. Your artistry has brought this story to life for every reader who picks this book up. Thank you to Whitney Bretzman, Casey Ward, Rustin Howard, Grace Larochelle, Sara Shepard, Steven Hennen, Katie Price, Rachel Iseman, Jackie Garcia, Lauren Huitt, Alison Curtin, Jim Smith, Deanna Gerard, and the entire B&T team. I feel proud and fortunate to be part of this family. And thank you to fellow Paw Prints creators

Jesse Byrd, Mikki Hernandez, Britt Gondolfi, and Amanda Romanick for your camaraderie.

Thank you to Benée Knauer for your support of this book since the very beginning. To think of all the conversations, brainstorming, and chapter summaries you put me through before I could even start writing! Your editorial genius and friendship have meant so much to me through this bumpy journey of writing and publishing two books. I can't picture writing a third without your emotional support and encouragement. And thank you to your entire family, especially Renny Gonzalez, for making me feel so welcome. Also, thank you to Victoria Sanders and Bernadette Baker-Baughman for your initial support and allowing me to incubate this idea.

Thank you to my beautiful family: Susan and James Carollo, Doug and Dennissee Carollo, the Colons, Sara Tawney, Claudia and Gene Devany, Diana Cherryholmes, and the entire Simonnetti, Ramos, and Tawney units.

Thank you to my friends and colleagues for all of your dedication, love, and support: Vishnu Pillai and the Pillai family, Ranley Duret, James Moongamakal, Dave Montpetit, Anthony Kang, Irene P. Eckert, Bhumika Vyas and the Vyas family, Ethan Rosen, Derek Caruso, Jesse Gaccione, Budd Burton Moss, Siwon Park (and Mama Joy), Hyeji and Brian Childs, Topher and Vanessa Hernandez, Amanda Uhle, Dave Eggers, Susan Shapiro, Donald Bogle, Christine and Ramón Martinez, Orrie Wolfer, Laura Catlan, Celine Leon, James Kim, Nancy Wong, Punita and Rahul Khanna, Betsy Bird, the entire Fordham University Press team, Jennifer Richards, Judy Yu, Rockwell Sands, Dave and Gina Pell, Neema Avashia, John Leguizamo, Wajahat Ai, Krishnendu Ray, Lidia and Tanya Bastianch, Jaswinder Bolina,

Claudia Forestieri, Vanessa Garcia, Richard Blanco, Junot Díaz, Carla Hall, Diana Liu, Greg Blank, Indo-American Arts Council, Peggy and William Low, Maureen Haynes Starr, Winston Chiang, Latinx in Publishing, Mitchell Kaplan, Tom Finkel, Alex Chester-Iwata, and MonaLisa Leung Beckford. There are many more names I'm probably leaving out so please forgive me if I've forgotten to thank you.

Thank you to my pets (aka co-workers) for their love and limitless joy: Maisie-Mae, Leo, Gizmo, Jake, and Oliver. And to those who left us in the past few years: Henry, Finn, Alfie, Brewster, and George.

Thank you to every library, bookstore, and education institution that has ever welcomed me and my work. Thank you to every editor, journalist, and producer who has ever given me an opportunity to tell my story. I'm forever grateful for the kindness and support of others who have taken a chance on a passionate weirdo like me.

Lastly, thank you to the teachers who ever saw a glimmer of potential in me. It's taken me a while to bloom, but I carry your encouragement with me every day.

If you've made it this far, thank you for reading *All Mixed Up*. Now, go out into the world and get dirty. Get creative. Find inspiration. Make mistakes. Live, live, live, my friends!

Raj

To learn more about Paw Prints
Publishing and to download a
discussion guide for this book,
please visit

pawprintspublishing.com